GILL JEPSON

OUT OF
TIME II

Raven's Hoard

GILL JEPSON

OUT OF TIME II

Raven's Hoard

Matador
9 Priory Business Park,
Wistow Road
Kibworth Beauchamp
Leicester LE8 0RX, UK
Tel: (+44) 116 279 2299
Fax: (+44) 116 279 2277
Email: books@troubador.co.uk
Web: www.troubador.co.uk / matador

ISBN 978 1780883 229

British Library Cataloguing in Publication Data.
A catalogue record for this book is available from the British Library.

Typeset in 11pt Palatino by Troubador Publishing Ltd, Leicester, UK
Printed and bound in Great Britain by TJ International, Padstow, Cornwall

Matador is an imprint of Troubador Publishing Ltd

*For Mum who always believed in me
and in memory of CS*

Locations in Raven's Hoard

Scales

• Ireleth
• Askam

Gleaston Castle
Water Mill
Beacon Hill

St Cuthberts of Aldingham
Moat Farm
Aldingham Motte

Dalton Castle

Abbot's Wood
Leece
Goadsbarrow

Furness Abbey
Bow Bridge
Mines
Roose

Point of Comfort

Barrow-in-Furness

St Michaels church

Sarah Beck

St Georges church

Concle Inn
Rampside

Conkin Bank

Roa

Foulney Island

Walney Island

Piel Island

www.gilljepson.co.uk

vi

CHAPTER 1

THE DIG

It was five-thirty in the morning and Nate had been awake for hours. It was the final straw. The tent was not only letting in copious amounts of rain, but the field was disappearing under a flood of gurgling mud and water, taking his tent with it. He was being swallowed alive by the field. Perhaps it was punishment for digging in it all summer. He sighed heavily as he rooted in the bottom of his haversack for his mobile phone. He dialled quickly and waited for the response.

"Yeah! It's me... I can't stay any longer, I'm drowning..."

Twenty minutes later he met her at the gate, bedraggled and frozen to the bones, with only his bag. He left the tent to its own fate and he didn't look back to see if it was still above water. As he got into the car, Chris appeared from the battered old caravan and waved.

"You off then?" he enquired.

"Yes, I'm frozen and I need a bath..." He looked down guiltily, as though he was deserting a sinking ship.

"You should've come and knocked at the caravan, I'd have taken pity on you... we don't expect you to drown for us, y'know!"

Nate's mum laughed. "I expect he was too proud to ask…"

"Or too daft!" exclaimed the grizzled old archaeologist, shaking his head.

Nate wished his Mum wouldn't be so friendly. He was easily embarrassed, he didn't want Chris to think he was still a kid; after all it was nearly three years since he'd joined the dig and he was fifteen now. He remembered that day well.

He'd seen a notice in the local paper, inviting people to visit the dig at the Water Mill, and Mum had agreed to take him. She knew he was interested in archaeology and to be truthful, so was she. So they drove down the lanes to the little village of Gleaston. It was a scary journey as usual, with Mum in the driving seat. She wasn't used to the narrow farm track and the second-hand car she drove was much too big for her. This led to some erratic manoeuvring and at times they veered into the hedgerows a little too closely.

They finally screeched into the gravel car park, drawing to a very abrupt, yet lucky halt at the edge of the river running along its perimeter. He got out quickly, trying not to look at the shocked people they had passed in the car park as they skidded through. She got out, seemingly oblivious to her unpredictable parking methods.

They walked over to the old Water Mill, joining the small crowd forming by the huge wheel. It was slowly turning and creaking, mesmerising everyone who was watching it. The sky was heavy with leaden, grey clouds; oppressive as only a thundery British summer could be. Their attention was distracted from the weather by the appearance of a wiry, middle-aged man, dressed in an old-fashioned trench coat, with a cape affair around his shoulders. If the coat wasn't strange enough, it was accompanied by a pair of khaki shorts and boots. He sported a drooping white moustache and his hair was sparse and prematurely white. Nate wondered how old he really was, because his face was not old, despite the white hair.

"I'm Chris Salter and for my sins I'm the archaeologist in charge of this dig. I hope you're prepared to get wet and muddy... and I hope you've brought your money with you... because we need it!" He shot a quick grin at them and turned on his heels and began pacing towards the field.

The tour had been interesting and it all looked very exciting. There were tents and a caravan circling a mess tent and benches. A St George's flag flapping in the breeze made the camp resemble a medieval camp at Agincourt. Chris was a real character, he called a spade a spade... he was incredibly blunt. He was an enigma, eccentric even. Immediately Nate was drawn to him, recognising similar qualities in himself. He hoped to be able to speak to him and ask if he wanted any volunteers, but felt too shy.

Mum saved the day by virtually telling his life story.

"He's always had a passion for archaeology ever since he saw 'Indiana Jones and the Last Crusade.' On and on she went.

He wriggled with embarrassment, but noticed that although Chris was nodding in the right places, he was not completely listening to Mum.

Chris watched Nate's reactions closely, and suddenly turned away from his Mum and barked, "So, young man, are *you* telling me you want to become part of my dig?" He looked straight at him with his piercing blue eyes, seeming to search his soul for the answer. Mum took the hint and shut up at last.

"Why… yes, if that's ok."

Chris studied him. The rain had started falling heavily and bounced off the canvas of the tent. It felt as if time had stopped.

"Well, as a rule, I don't have children on my digs, but so long as you promise you can be sensible and do as you're told, we could give it a go. You can come tomorrow and I'll introduce you to everyone."

"Brilliant! Thanks… I'll be here!" exclaimed Nate.

"Bring your lunch and waterproofs and be prepared for some hard graft… you seem to have something about you… we'll see anyway."

That was how it happened. How he became involved with the dig, with Chris and with the mission.

Chapter 2

The Find

Nate didn't return to the dig for a few days. He really couldn't face the thought of trying to salvage his tent and belongings in this rain and wind. When he did go back at the weekend, he rode down on his bike. It was still breezy, but blue skies were chasing away the dark rain clouds. He reached the dig field by eleven and Chris and the others were already about their business. As he propped his bike up against the field gate, he could see them all waving and pointing. He drew nearer and prepared himself for a barrage of insults and jeers because he had left during the storm.

"Did he melt in that rain then?"

"Bless him, he's back... hope he's got an umbrella!"

He shrugged off the hail of good-natured insults and teasing. Chris strolled over and greeted him.

"Glad to see you back... hoped it hadn't put you off. I'm afraid it's an occupational hazard... rain, mud, more rain and trench foot!" He grinned and turned away, beckoning him to follow.

They walked to a far corner of the field where another digger was working in a narrow trench which had been put in already and a few meagre finds were in the seed tray beside it.

"You can work here today, I need Darren on the other side of the leet," he said.

The leet was a man-made branch of the river, which actually forced water in the opposite direction to the real watercourse, down to the Water Mill. It provided an obvious boundary for the archaeologists to use to partition the field into sections.

Nate got down to business quickly, using a piece of old tarpaulin as a kneeler. He picked up the small trowel that Darren had abandoned and began painstakingly scraping the surface of the exposed ground. Each time he hit a stone or rock he picked it up and examined it closely to see if it was a find or not. The sun grew hotter and soon he was sweating. He wiped his forehead and began to realise why all archaeologists seemed to wear eccentric head gear, from Indiana Jones to Phil Harding from Time Team. Whatever the weather, a hat was a definite requirement. He must get one soon, somehow a baseball cap didn't seem right.

He had been working for an hour, his neck and shoulders were aching and his knees were stiff and numb from kneeling. All he had turned up were a few teeth, probably from an animal, and a couple of pieces of orange-coloured pottery, which he could now identify as medieval. In fact it was nothing very exciting or remarkable. He straightened his back and stretched his neck and looked across the field towards the tents. Chris called across the field, "Tea up!"

Everyone was moving towards the mess tent for lunch. Paul, another young digger, shouted over to him to join them. With relief he stood up and stretched again and walked over the wooden bridge to the other side of the field. He stopped to wash the dirt from his hands in the fast-running stream and wiped them down the sides of his jeans to dry them. When he reached the trestle-tables, roughly set for lunch, he nodded to the others who were already sitting down ready to eat.

It was a good lunch today, thick vegetable soup, brim full of whole new potatoes, with huge hunks of fresh bread. Something about being out in a field made your appetite keener and made the food tastier and more filling. It was all washed down with steaming mugs of tea. Feeling as full as a drum, Nate sat in the tatty old armchair and sat back, listening to the conversation around the table.

Very soon the conversation came round to local tales and stories, some of them very tall. Chris always had lots of tales to tell. There were stories about the caves at Scales, where the remains of ancient dwellers had been found, alongside their discarded flint tools. They were regaled with tales of invaders and battles, the monks at Furness Abbey, marauding Scots and Henry Vlll's destruction of the abbey. He had so much knowledge and Nate tried hard to remember everything he told them. Nate hoped that one day the tales would be useful to him, when he became a famous archaeologist! He would never guess just how useful they would be… and how much he would depend upon them in time.

The next day a visitors' tour arrived promptly at one. The group was a mixed bag of people, from young to old, and one could only guess why many of them were here. Some seemed more interested in visiting the mill and having a coffee than tramping round the field. However, one man stood out. He was taller than the rest and stood quietly at the back. Chris obviously knew him, as he grunted a greeting to him. The man nodded in acknowledgement and smiled, but the smile did not reach his eyes. There was apparently no love lost between the two.

They wandered across the field and the visitors were herded around like errant sheep by Nate at the back, ensuring that they did not stray too far, or disturb any of the diggers too much. However, the slick gentleman followed him closely. As the tour came to an end, two elderly ladies engaged Chris in deep and lengthy conversation. He kept a weather eye on Nate and the man turned to face him.

"So, you have an interest in archaeology, young man?" he asked.

Nate shrugged. Pretty obvious that – he wouldn't be here, would he, if he wasn't?

"You will learn nothing here, you know. This old fool is out of his depth!" he stated baldly.

Nate was taken aback. How dare he?

"You would learn far more with me. I have a very important dig at Aldingham, in a field near the dairy farm. We have professionals on tap, funding from the University and weekly work experience. Our finds are amazing and we can promise you an exciting experience."

He smiled and preened himself. He made Nate feel uncomfortable and mad at the same time.

"I'm fine, thanks!" retorted Nate.

The man's manner changed. His steely eyes bored into him and he sneered, an unpleasant and sinister glare distorting his face.

"You are a fool!" His face contorted with anger.

"Whoa! What's your problem, mate?" said Darren the digger, as he ran over to intervene.

The man turned his cold gaze on him.

"You are a fool too! You have had the same offer and yet you choose to remain with this old charlatan!" he spat.

"I don't know about that! But I know who I prefer to work with!"

"And *I* don't appreciate being called a charlatan Silas Dixon!" interjected Chris, who had finally extricated himself from the two ladies.

"Salter! You are a bumbling old fool and have no right to seek the treasures – they are ours and we will be the ones to find them."

With that, he turned on his heels and left.

"Nasty piece of work!" hissed Darren.

"Hmm! A troubled soul to be sure!" added Chris. "But he has no more chance of finding treasure than you do of reaching the moon!"

Nate had not realised that such rivalry existed in archaeology and it kind of amused him; cool, it was just like when Indiana and the French archaeologist were pitted against each other in "Raiders of the Lost Ark".

They went back to camp and started making tea. Everyone relaxed and as they shared food and stories a lull fell over the gathering. Later that evening Chris drew out an object from his caravan and walked across to Nate. In his hand he carried a battered old fedora – just like the one that Indiana Jones had worn. Darren guffawed with laughter as Chris unceremoniously dropped it on to Nate's head. He adjusted it, thrilled to receive it, even if it was a bit grubby and worn.

"I thought you deserved this after today! Call it a badge of honour, and it gives you excellent protection from the sun. Everyone knows all diggers have a special hat!" he grinned, as though he had known what Nate had been thinking earlier.

CHAPTER 3

SMUGGLERS INN 1750

The night was bleak and cold. Rain drove across the sands and stung Tom full in the face like needles. He kicked his horse's flanks to encourage him on through the storm and the great black beast champed at the bit and snorted in protest. He knew he had to keep going, everything depended on it, especially Dolly's safe keeping.

He had to reach the Concle Inn at all costs – now they knew the cache was discovered, they would be making their way back to the inn to demand answers. He had been stupid to jeopardise Dolly and her father, just to take the smugglers red-handed. He might have known that the risks were too high! The weather worked against him; wind and rain seared his face and tore at his cloak, which flew out behind him like a ship's tarpaulin. Ice-cold rain pricked his eyes, forcing them shut; he brushed his face with the back of his hand and focused on the lane ahead. His horse snorted, panting noisily, and Tom could feel him straining as he urged him on into the night.

The village was in darkness, with a slight glimmer of light escaping from one of the fisherman's cottages. Horse and rider splashed through the mud, becoming one, with but a single purpose. The waves roared and leapt over the edge of the road, clutching with watery claws at the travellers as they hurtled past. The Concle Inn came into view, crouching like a brooding animal on the edge of the shoreline, challenging him to enter.

The inn was shrouded in darkness, no sounds escaping from within. Tom leapt from his horse and tethered her behind the barn. He sank back into the shadows and watched the doorway. The rain swept across the yard in sheets and the wooden sign creaked and rattled, the hinges straining. Tom pulled down his hat and wrapped his cloak tightly around him; he ducked down low, running quickly across the courtyard to the inn wall. Tom's heart was pounding like a mighty hammer as he shrank against the wall below the window. He could make out gruff voices through the pane and his heart jumped into his mouth when he heard a cry. They had Dolly!

Dolly sat bolt upright on the small stool before the fire, facing the angry men. Voices were raised and she looked them in the eye defiantly despite their anger. Her father looked on nervously, eyes darting from Dolly to her furious inquisitors.

"What did ye see, girl? We must know!" cried the man with the heavy jowls and lank hair. Gabriel Swarbrick was well known to her, both as a local fisherman and notorious troublemaker. He scowled threateningly.

"I don't know what you mean!" she replied bravely, her thin voice betraying her fear.

"For God's sake, child, answer," her father pleaded.

Dolly remained silent.

Swarbrick lurched towards her, grabbing her slim shoulders and shaking her like a rag doll. She rocked on the wooden stool, almost falling. His face contorted with fury and became crimson. His fury was short – lived as he was suddenly winded and knocked nearly senseless to the slate floor. Tom rained blows upon Gabriel with a fury he had never felt before. Swarbrick's companions, stunned at first, leapt to his aid and dragged the lad away. When he got his breath back Swarbrick screamed, "Get them into the pit! We'll deal with them later!" He wiped his bloody mouth roughly with the back of his hand. "Make haste! We have the tide to catch or we'll lose our chance!"

The two burly men lifted the young pair off their feet as easily as if they were bags of straw. Their protests were muffled by grubby large hands over their mouths and their struggles were in vain. Dolly's father, John, reached helplessly for his young daughter, but to no avail. Swarbrick hit him full in the face, sending him flying across the slate flags. "That's a taster of what you'll get if you let her and that Preventive man go while we are away!"

With that he followed the others through the trapdoor near the fireplace. The pit had been hewn from the rock and formed a cavern of surprising proportions. Dolly and Tom knew of its existence but had never seen it before. The cave was used for cock-fighting, where local smugglers and pirates gambled their ill-gotten gains. The bloody evidence of the cruel sport could be seen, russet stains daubing the gravel floor. Empty rum bottles lay abandoned around the edge and kegs and barrels were stacked at the back of the room.

The two young people resisted their captor's attempt to tie them, but the wiry youth called Charnley drew a filleting knife from his belt and pointed it menacingly at Dolly's throat. He did not need to speak, the message was clear. They were bound together with rope and abandoned in the dark as the last chink of light was extinguished as the trapdoor was closed shut. Silence enveloped them like a heavy cloak. The silence was broken by small sobs from Dolly. Tom felt helpless. He tried to move his arms but the rope bonds tightened and prevented him. They took in their surroundings, seeing dark shapes and a slim shaft of pale light from the trapdoor above as their eyes grew used to the dark.

"I'm sorry, Dolly. I should have waited 'til they had gone, but I couldn't watch them harm you," whispered Tom.

"It i'nt your fault Tom… if anyone's to blame, 'tis me dad fer lettin' 'em use the inn," she sniffed. "What can we do to get out?"

He wriggled and shuffled in answer. This only served to upset her further and she began crying. They fell silent. Suddenly Tom shifted his position and cried out.

"Right! Try and shuffle over to the corner."

Dolly tried to twist around so she could see what the corner had to offer.

"Come on… shuffle over!" insisted Tom.

The two pushed and slid over the rough floor. It was uncomfortable and surprisingly hard work, but they managed to reach their target.

"Now, we need to turn round the other way," Tom instructed.

The pair twisted round. Dolly heard a clink. Tom had moved them to where two bottles had been discarded. He manoeuvred his hands until he could grip one of the bottles.

"Now, keep still while I try and break this. If you move you'll cut yourself."

Dolly held her breath and tightened all her muscles to prevent her moving. The first attempt failed, merely sending the bottle spinning away. On the second attempt, the bottle hit a sharp stone and cracked. With a little more pressure it broke in half, splinters of glass pricking the side of Tom's hand.

"Ow!" he exclaimed. "That hurt but at least 'tis broken and sharp."

Dolly relaxed and leaned against his back, supporting him as he sawed the broken glass across the rope bindings.

It was hot and slow progress, but finally the rope frayed enough for Tom to snap the bindings.

The pair moved apart, stretching and rubbing their wrists. Tom undid the rope around his ankles, jumped up and untied Dolly too.

"So, what dost thou suggest now?" Dolly asked. "How do we get out of here?"

"I know not. I will try the trapdoor," he answered.

He pushed and rattled the door, but it was locked tight. The cellar was difficult to negotiate and they bumped into casks and objects as they moved. They explored the outer perimeter of the cavernous room, feeling their way with their hands. Tom stumbled as his hands reached into a recess in the rocks. At the back of the recess was a groove. Tom felt up and down the slot until he found a metal ring at the base.

"What is it? What have you found?" asked Dolly excitedly.

"'Tis a ring, I think I can pull it!"

He knelt and gripped the ring and pulled with all his might. Nothing happened. This time instead of pulling, he tried to lift it. Again, nothing changed. With renewed vigour he heaved the ring as hard as he could. His effort stole his balance and he fell forward, pushing the ring back into the groove. A loud click snapped the silence. The pair listened. A low growling came from behind the wall and slowly it rolled backwards, grinding to a halt only a metre or so behind the room they were in. A light breeze flickered from behind the wall, encouraging them to go on. Tom grabbed Dolly's hand and pulled her through the gap. They slipped around the false wall and as they stepped on to the floor behind, a board released the lever which had first opened it, closing firmly.

"I pray we can get out of here," whispered Dolly.

"The door must lead somewhere," answered Tom.

Dolly kept her doubts to herself and hoped that he was right. They stumbled along the narrow passage, feeling their way and following the increasingly stronger breeze.

The tunnel seemed clearer as they progressed, shapes becoming more visible. Suddenly, as they reached a bend, a gust of rain-filled wind took their breath away. They could see an opening. More than that, they could hear the sea. They quickened their pace and a pale light from outside traced the outline of the exit. It was concealed with overgrown vegetation and rocks, not easily visible from outside.

"We must be careful now… we don't know who's about," whispered Tom urgently.

Dolly nodded in acknowledgement. They dropped down, bending low to crawl through the hole. The ground rose as they scrambled out, the wind whipping their hair and clothes viciously. The rain stung like nettles and Dolly was soon shivering in the cold. Tom took off his cloak and wrapped it round her thin shoulders. They had emerged above the Conkin Bank, presently covered by a wild and raging sea. They looked around, checking they were still alone, and with a single will ran across the muddy banking and through the windswept trees into the fields. They ran as fast as they could over the rough ground. They found themselves on the path to St Michael's church. The weather worked against them, wind blasting and buffeting them like sails on a ship, rain pelting them with an icy assault. As they stumbled on, Tom's feet became heavier and heavier with the mud. He slowed to a halt, his boots sinking into a slick of sodden clay. The two wobbled as they pulled their feet free of the gluey mire. Dolly quivered and slowly slid backwards, falling into the bog.

"Urgh! It's filthy! I am drenched."

"Come!" cried Tom, "thou must get up!"

He dragged her to her feet and the mud slurped as her heavy skirts separated from the mess. They trudged on, aiming for the silhouette of the church in the distance. Light was breaking weakly in the east, lightening the billowing black clouds. They knew they must reach safety before dawn, before they could be seen, before their captors knew they were missing. The pathway wound its way past the graveyard and on to the cart track towards Roose village. Their destination lay some miles beyond this, in the hamlet of Leece. They were exhausted but could not slacken their pace for fear of discovery. Finally they reached the edge of the village, running faster as they reached their target. They hammered at the low wooden door of the cottage.

No light came from within, all was silent.

"We must go in!" insisted Tom.

They pushed open the door and closed it behind them heavily. They had reached their haven.

CHAPTER 4

JEFFREY

It was the summer holidays again and time to go down to the dig. Nate was made up! He loved the camaraderie and sense of purpose he got from being part of the dig. It was the time he always felt best about himself. They were going to be busy because they were exploring a fresh piece of ground nearer to the castle – or what was left of it. He loved Gleaston castle. It was everything it should be, crumbling, imposing, mysterious. The farm was built amongst it and from its stones, but there was still an impressive keep and extensive curtain wall. It was the second castle built by the Le Fleming family and had been built in the thirteenth century. They outgrew the first one at Aldingham.

That one fascinated Nate too. He loved its conical mound or motte as it was called. He admired the viewpoint it had overlooking Morecambe Bay and the way that it still dominated the landscape. He could spot hints of earthworks and archaeology visible on the field surface and was pleased that there was still a farm below it even after all the centuries that had passed. Mote Farm was a splendid late medieval farm with the remnants of a moat. He knew one day he wanted to explore it all and make some sense of what he could see.

He stood for a time by the gate into the dig field, gazing at the encampment. His reverie was disturbed by the growling of a motorbike coming up behind him. A helmeted and goggled figure drew into the gateway and turned off the engine. He climbed from his steed like an erstwhile knight. Nate grinned. The rider removed the old-fashioned helmet and goggles revealing Chris's weather-worn features. He nodded in acknowledgement and turned to the stationary bike, removing a wooden box from the carrier at the back. Without a word he walked towards the gate and opened it. The two of them walked towards the camp, silently.

Chris dropped the box on to the trestle-table. Nate wondered what was in it, but didn't like to ask. Very soon he was kneeling in a muddy trench, scraping the topsoil away carefully, hoping to reveal an amazing new treasure. Hours passed and his knees ached, his wrist cramped and became stiff where he had held the trowel in the same position. His meagre finds were visible in the seed tray and to him did not seem impressive. There were a couple of animal teeth, a scattering of flint chippings and two small pieces of red medieval pottery.

They were similar to everyone else's, so he felt reassured. After the banquet that was their evening meal they began exchanging stories. As usual Nate did more listening than talking. Soon, the subject turned to the box which Chris had placed on the table earlier. The suspense built as he lifted off the lid and with a flourish pulled out a human skull, like a magician pulling a rabbit from a top hat.

"Wow!" gasped Nate. "Where's that from?"

"Or more appropriately, who's it from?" chuckled Chris. "It's extremely old… and I like to call him… Jeffrey!"

"Where did it come from then?" asked Darren, the oldest of the diggers.

Well… there's a tale." He sighed and looked closely at the skull.

"Well? Go on then!" demanded Darren.

"Well, I'm not going to tell you – am I? I need to be sure I can trust you!" He fixed him with a steely glare.

Darren and the others laughed uneasily. Chris was often abrasive and it was difficult to know when he was being serious. He turned to Nate and suddenly threw the skull to him. Luckily he caught it nimbly, thanking his lucky stars for his rugby training.

"What do you make of that then, lad?" he growled.

Still shocked at having a skull thrown at him, he raised his eyebrows. He held it in his hands and looked closely at it.

"Ha, alas poor Yoric – eh, Nate?" guffawed Darren.

"Leave the lad alone!" Chris barked.

Feeling hot under the collar, Nate looked again at this remnant of humanity and found himself wondering who he might have been. He was drawn to the shape of the head, followed the contours with his fingers, and peered at the teeth. He stopped and took a breath. On the left side of the skull, from the orbit of the eye to the top of the jaw bone, was a split or groove. He rotated it slowly and discovered another split at the base of the skull as though a piece had been splintered from it. He ran his finger along the ragged edge, debating whether to speak.

"Well? What do you see?" asked Chris.

"Er... there's like a split... here." He indicated the cheekbone. "Then there's a chunk broken off at the back – like it's all jagged... and look – there's a hole on the temple as well!"

"And what does that mean?" quizzed Chris further.

Nate shrugged. "Erm... I think... I think that this man has been battered with something?"

"Yes, I concur with that. What type of battery and what sort of weapon do you think?"

"I think some sort of axe or sword? Or maybe both? Summat with a sharp edge anyway!" offered Nate.

"Well done!" Chris turned to the others and grinned. "Good observation skills for a young 'un! He has been slashed from the front by a blade, stabbed in the temple with a sharp object – maybe an axe or mace handle, and finally the injury at the back could... *could* indicate he has been beheaded!"

"But who is it?" pressed Nate.

"Ah well, that may be something we can't establish... at the moment!"

Without any further discussion, Chris seized the skull and replaced it into the box, closing the lid firmly. Everyone knew that the conversation was at an end.

As Nate lay in his tent that night, staring at the stars through the gap he had left open, he went over the day's events in his head. He was intrigued to discover who the skull belonged to and how and why he had died. He couldn't help thinking that Chris knew more than he was letting on. Where on earth had he found it? Surely not near the castle, they would have noticed. Where could it have come from? After all, Chris rode up with it on his motorbike, so he had brought it from somewhere.

His dreaming was broken by the sound of scuffling outside. He froze momentarily, listening, ears pricked like a dog. Another sound echoed across the field. Someone had knocked over a metal bucket which was next to the caravan. He breathed a sigh of relief. It must be Chris up and about. He glanced at his mobile phone to check the time. It was 4.15 am. Too early for Chris to be up then! Further noises came from near the van. This time he sat bolt upright. His breath was short and rapid. He clambered out of his sleeping bag and scrambled to the opening of the tent. Carefully he peeled back the flap and looked through.

A shadowy figure stood in the doorway of the caravan. He moved into the van. Without a second thought, Nate leapt out of his tent and raced towards the caravan, shouting at the top of his voice.

The figure jumped and turned. Nate couldn't make out who it was, but his reaction confirmed that whoever it was, he should not be there. He jumped from the van, rocking it as he did so, and landed on the grass, momentarily losing his footing. He ran away from Nate, who was in hot pursuit. By this time Chris had emerged from the van and the other diggers had begun to appear from tents along the field like moles, feeling their way in the dark. Torch beams swung round the field like searchlights, illuminating bushes and objects which looked unearthly in the dark.

The man had disappeared over the gate in the confusion and a car engine roared into life and vanished down the narrow lane beyond the mill. Lamps were lit all round the camp and everyone was huddling round the caravan. Chris stood on the top step of the caravan. He looked older than usual and weary. His white hair stood in tufts on his head giving him the appearance of an exotic bird of prey. He looked around the gathered diggers, as if he was silently taking a roll call. Everyone was there.

"What happened? What did he want?" clamoured Mel, one of the young volunteers.

"Money – they'd be after money…" cried Paul.

"Or they might think we had treasure – digs down south are always being raided for gold and stuff!" suggested Darren.

"Why would they think we had gold or treasure?" countered Mel scornfully, ruffling her short dark hair.

"Somebody may believe we have found something valuable! But not necessarily gold or money," explained Chris plainly. "Maybe someone has been talking about our finds!"

"Oh yeah! Like Nate's boar's teeth or those flints? Maybe it's that archaeologist over at Aldingham – he's always seemed a bit shifty to me," laughed Darren.

"Well, someone means business! *Someone* found us interesting and *someone* believes we have found *something*!"

He looked directly at Nate. His blue eyes seemed to be telling him something.

Something, which would need to be spoken of in time.

It did not take long for the time to be right. Towards the end of the dig Chris beckoned Nate to come over to him. They sat at the mess table, facing each other. Chris stared intently at Nate, his crinkly blue eyes full of unspoken words. Nate would normally have felt uncomfortable under such scrutiny, but he merely relaxed and looked straight into Chris's clear blue eyes. He found melancholy there which he could not quite fathom. Tranquillity had surrounded them, bathing them in a still peace. Time almost stood still and the diggers in the field became insignificant, and all that could be heard was the constant burble of the stream, running on eternally.

"You have a task to fulfil," said Chris plainly.

Nate's face crumpled with confusion, unsure of what Chris meant.

"You must save an important, sacred treasure. It's imperative that you find it. I can help, but I won't be here for…" His voice trailed off ominously.

Nate wracked his brains to understand what treasure he could possibly be referring to. Even Chris wouldn't call the few finds of flint, pottery and bone that they had found treasure.

Chris reached beneath the table and placed the battered finds box containing Jeffrey on to the table in front of Nate. He opened it and lifted out the skull, holding it in front of him.

"These are the remains of Oswald, King of the Northumbrians. He was slaughtered by the heathen King Penda and his parts spread across the four kingdoms of the north. A raven stole away his sacred arm and where it fell a holy spring grew. His sacred bones and the sword which killed this saintly warrior were saved by his brother and rested safely for many a year at the abbey of Bardney. The heathen Northmen overran Bardney and the relics were ransacked. A red – haired devil found the sword that took brave Oswald's head from his shoulders; he fled with his spoils and the sword was lost. Oswald's bones were taken to abbeys far and wide; but his skull rested secretly at Furness Abbey until the great dissolution. It is believed that the skull lay in St Cuthbert's tomb at Durham, carried there during the great progress of that saint's body, but it was instead left at Furness for safe keeping." He spoke strangely and sombrely.

Nate was astounded and he fixed his eyes on the skull which had been so irreverently named Jeffrey.

"But how can you know this? How did you get the skull, Chris, if it came from the abbey?" he interjected.

"When the abbey was destroyed, some sought to protect and secure the treasures within. 'Tisn't the only treasure to be in peril at this time, but others are assigned to those items. My ancestors were abbey masons and as such swore a great oath to keep God's treasures safe. Some were known by the name Mason, but my forefathers lived on the marshes and worked the salt pans on the plain and were named for their trade."

Nate had never given much thought to where Chris's name Salter had come from and this was a revelation. Weird!

"We knew the ebb and flow of the tides, the secret tracks across the sands and the old ways to harvest the sea. We did this until our livelihoods were sold by the fat king, Henry, and squandered on those who had not earned it. The lands were sold to make rich men more powerful. They craved those treasures protected by the abbey and it became our undertaking to recover and conceal as many as we could. The skull was but one. The sword which smote this sacred head is yet another and one which is in peril in *this* time."

Chris stopped speaking and looked meaningfully at Nate. He was unsure how he should respond and cleared his throat uneasily.

"Wow! I don't know what to say... how does this involve me then?"

"You too have kin who will help the abbey protect its treasure."

Nate remained unconvinced but humoured Chris. Really, he was beginning to think the old boy had lost it. All this about abbeys and treasure... it all sounded a bit far fetched.

He rose from his bench and was about to rejoin the others in the field. Chris stood too, smiling strangely.

"You'll see, lad, you'll see."

Nate shrugged and walked towards where Mel and Darren were working. He called to them and waved. They didn't move or call back. Odd? They must surely have heard him. He yelled again, louder this time. Suddenly the small hairs on the back of his neck and his arms stood up and he shuddered involuntarily. They were stock still, each one of them. In fact *everything* was stock still – the sheep, Mick at the mill emptying his bin, a car in the road... and a sparrow mid flight, suspended in thin air, frozen in time. His flesh grew cold and clammy; he jumped as he felt a hand upon his shoulder.

Chris smiled.

"It's a smart trick, isn't it?" he asked, not expecting an answer.

"Did you do this? Did you make everything stop?" Nate croaked uneasily.

"We needed some time to talk, uninterrupted… so I gave us some. It's something which has come in useful many times."

"Who are you?" asked Nate, looking at him as though for the first time. The scruffy, curmudgeonly archaeologist had disappeared and in his place Chris took on the mantle of a wise man of many years' experience. It was him, but ancient wisdom shone through his eyes like a beacon.

"I am who you know, but I am more than that, I *am* my ancestors and bear their duty to the abbey and its precious treasures. You must not be afraid. I have but little time and you must listen and follow my instructions."

Nate listened.

"I have directions for you. You must seek an ancient map, which will take you along perilous roads 'til you find what you seek."

"But what *do* I seek?"

"Oswald's sword, 'twas hidden close by a great hoard," answered Chris.

"It was found, but is lost again. There are those who would take it for themselves. Beware, for they will stop at nothing to seize it."

"Where is the map? How will I find it?" pressed Nate.

"You must go to the Motte. You may find what you seek there. But have a care, the road you embark upon is full of danger."

Time began to whirr into life once more and a solitary raven glided down from the trees and landed on the top of the mess tent.

Chapter 5

The Parting

Nate sat in the passenger seat of his Mum's car, listening to the prattling voice of the woman they were taking with them to Grange. He was inwardly fuming that she was intruding and the way she was going on and on, he wanted to shout out. It wasn't her fault but he was mad. Ironically, it was a sunny day, wasn't it always the way? It had been exactly the same when they had been to Granddad's funeral last summer, hot and sunny. What was that all about? But the night he died, those few weeks ago – *that* was something different; he had died in the midst of a violent storm, thunder, lightening, the lot! Like the Viking gods were calling him, each thunder clap – a blow from Thor's hammer! He would never forget it...Thursday (Thor's day). Now he had to contend with Chris as well. Two people he relied on and believed in gone without a single thought for him!

They drew up outside the Victorian church and parked. He sat next to Mum in the wooden pew and fiddled with the order of service, so much that the hymn book fell from the ledge and fell with a clatter to the floor. He sighed ponderously and picked it up. He gazed at the front of the chapel and looked at the simple lines of the wood and masonry. He almost cried out in surprise as he recognised his maths tutor in front. He turned round and nodded politely at Mum and then winked at Nate. He could see a row full of archaeologists and historians that he had met at the dig and the usual crew were there too. He let a huge sigh escape again.

Everyone stood as the mourners and the coffin came in. The family stood in the pew at the front and then the minister began the service. Time stood still for Nate. The service informed him of many things he had been unaware of, but each one made him feel his loss more keenly. The more he heard, the more remarkable he knew Chris had been. A tear stung his eye and his bottom lip trembled. His throat ached with unshed tears and he stood tall and straight. Mum sniffed into a tissue and the rest of the congregation looked as sad as he was. It was weird looking at the box in the aisle and imagining his friend inside.

It was incomprehensible to think he would not see or hear him again. Incomprehensible and… and crap! Anger twisted his heart, wringing out the anguished tears and spilling them down his red cheeks. His shoulders shook with grief and he became so absorbed in trying NOT to cry that he didn't hear another word of the service. He sniffed and wiped his nose on his tissue.

When it was all over they stood in the car park for a time, talking to the other mourners. It was better outside, not quite so intense, and soon he and Darren were sharing memories together of the dig and things that Chris had said and done. Darren took off his jacket and went to his car. He delved into the boot for a moment and returned with a familiar object. It was Jeffrey, and a letter.

"Chris wanted you to have these – said you'd know what to do with 'em. God knows what you'll do with a smelly old skull! I'd donate it to the museum or something!" Even as he spoke the words, Darren knew that was the last thing Nate would do.

Nate took the box and the letter silently to the car and sat with it on his knee. The chatty woman got in the back, chirping on about a lovely service and how nice it had been. She went on and on until they dropped her off at the top of her lane. He breathed a sigh of relief when she got out and was not sorry to see her go.

When they got home tea was ready. Dad had made spaghetti bolognese. Well, that was one bright spot in an otherwise horrible day – at least Mum wasn't cooking. He felt better after the meal and went to retrieve the box from the car. Naturally his brother and sister clamoured to see what was inside. He wasn't really ready to share with anyone and he reacted grumpily

"Come on, wally! Lets 'ave a look," pestered his older brother Rob. "Go on! You know it makes sense!" he continued in a fake cockney accent. He was so irritating at times, he really was asking for a thump!

"Leave him alone, Rob! He doesn't want to!" interrupted Rebecca sensitively.

"What is it? Go on! I only want to see," Rob insisted. He made a grab for the box and Nate swung away quickly, catching Rebecca on the chin with his elbow.

"Ow! For God's sake, Nate!" she cried, rubbing her chin.

Rob lurched for the box again, unbalancing the three of them and sending the box flying across the room, the contents falling on to the carpet.

The skull rolled to a halt at Rebecca's feet, landing facing her, its lower jaw separating and producing a macabre grin. She shrieked and leapt on to the chair. Mum and Dad rushed in from the kitchen to find their daughter crying, the boys wrestling on the floor and a skull staring sightlessly up at them. Mum looked as if she would faint and dad wacked both boys with the tea towel, separating them.

"What *is* going on? You're like a couple of nursery kids you two! And what are you skriking, about Becca?"

"Well, it's a dead person's head – 's not very nice in your living room, is it?"

The cacophony of noise was quelled by Mum picking up the offending object and replacing it in the box.

"Well, I'm sorry Nate, but I can't have that in the house, no matter who gave it to you," she shivered. "It's morbid and probably full of germs. It needs to go in the shed, NOW!"

Nate knew better than to argue and he didn't trust Mum not to get the Dettol out to disinfect Jeffrey if he didn't move him quickly.

Rob sniggered and whispered "Loser" under his breath as he walked past. This provoked a kick and another short scuffle, until Dad reprimanded them again.

Nate reflected for a moment in the shed. He took out the letter and quietly read its contents.

My friend,

I told you that day at the dig that I didn't have much time and although I can slow down time, I have no power over the end of a life and when its time runs out. I leave you Jeffrey - you know his true identity and must guard him until the other treasure is found. He will guide and remind you of the quest and I will help you in time... but I cannot say when or how. Be vigilant and trust only those who prove their worth. Evil forces are around you and will watch for your movements - use time to help you and learn from it... I will be there with you in spirit

Your true friend
Crispin Salter

Crispin? He had no idea that Chris was short for Crispin. In fact he had never heard the name before. What on earth did that mean – he would help him "in time"? He'd have a job! How could he possibly help from the grave? No! It was up to him now. Chris was gone and he must complete the quest – no matter what! As he locked the shed, he noticed a lonely raven perched on the tree behind, its glittering eyes staring knowingly at him. If he didn't know any better he would have thought it was the same one from the dig.

CHAPTER 6

WEIRD STUFF

Nate spent a restless night. It was humid, as late summer sometimes was, and he felt uneasy and apprehensive. He put it down to the upset over Chris today and the fact that it had all brought up the sadness of losing Granddad too. He finally dropped off into a fitful sleep, which left him tired and irritable next day. He got up late, coming down to a scene of destruction.

Something had got into the back garden and tipped up all the pots and wrecked the place. His sister had been sent to Gran's to get some spare pots and she seemed a bit spooked. Probably still scared of the skull... the skull... oh no! He ran through the kitchen and out to the shed. Luckily it was still locked, but all around it were scores and scratches as though an animal had tried to get in. Around the base of the shed were chunks of sandstone and dust – weird! Dad was sweeping up and told him to get the shovel.

He was puzzled and a little worried. Was the destruction because someone was after the skull? He suddenly remembered the night at the camp when they had all been disturbed. Perhaps this was the danger that Chris had warned of.

When they had finished clearing up, Nate unlocked the shed and checked the box. He knew he would have to find somewhere safer – but where?

The idea struck him later that day. Everyone was out. Mum had taken Rebecca and her friend Danny down to Furness Abbey for the afternoon, Dad was at work and Rob was playing football somewhere. It was inspired. He had been helping Dad to fix the slabs on the patio and they were almost finished. All that remained was to place the bird bath on the central stone and it would be done.

It didn't take him long to dig a hole in the centre of the patio. He dug furtively, feeling he was being watched. He was suspicious of everything, including the birds. He had noticed loads of magpies fluttering around earlier, but they seemed to have gone now. However, one bird did remain – the sleek, black raven. It sat perched on the hedge and peered at him curiously. He ignored it. It seemed benign enough and it couldn't be bad if it had been at the dig, could it? He was really cracking up! Birds weren't good or bad! They were… just birds. Weren't they?

He placed the finds box into a big polythene bag and tied the top. He hoped that this would protect the skull until he could find a better place. He hurriedly covered the hole with soil and replaced the slab and finally, with all the brute force he could muster, dragged the stone bird bath over and pushed it into place, concealing the hiding place fully. He stood back, admiring his work, and then set to, sweeping and tidying so that everywhere was clean. Not bad for an afternoon's work, a hidden treasure and brownie points for finishing a job without being asked!

The raven glided down from the hedge, and balanced on the rim of the bird bath and peered at Nate. It seemed to be offering its approval. He smirked at the thought, but then was shocked, as the bird jumped up on to his shoulder. He knew now that the bird was not any random bird, but rather was an ally.

Chapter 7

A safe haven

Dolly and Tom awoke early. Elias Sharpe had just returned from milking and had worked up an appetite. His mouselike wife, Sarah, scuttled about, busy preparing breakfast for her husband and the farm lad. The large kitchen table was big enough to seat them all comfortably. Sarah served up porridge, followed by bacon with newly made bread and butter. There was small beer to drink and everyone took a pewter pot to drink from. The pair ate hungrily. It seemed hours since their last meal and they fell upon the cured bacon like ravenous dogs. Sarah bustled about lifting her small babe from the ancient wooden cradle by the fire. She sat down on the wooden rocking chair and snuggled the child to her closely to feed him. She watched the proceedings, steadily rocking back and forth, with a hypnotic rhythm.

Elias wiped his mouth with the back of his huge hand. He let out a tremendous belch and took a swig from the tankard of ale before him.

"So, lad! What's happened to thee?" He turned to face Tom.

"We were caught by Swarbrick's crew! 'Twas troublesome to escape..." his voice tailed off as he remembered the brutal smugglers.

"Aye they're a bad lot, lad! But how hast tha got saddled with yon wench?" He waved his hand at Dolly.

Tom shot Dolly a swift glance, smiling quickly to reassure her.

"We have an understanding Elias"

"An understanding? Tha's on thin ice, lad! She's that crooked Jackson's bairn, tha can't trust her!" He shook his head solemnly. "And thee a Revenue man! 'Twill come to tears, mark my words!"

Dolly flushed, hot with embarrassment at his sour words. She looked him straight in the eye, challenging him.

"I won't betray Tom! We... care for each other!"

Tom smiled quietly. Elias ignored her statement and slowly filled his clay pipe with tobacco. He sucked on the pipe as he lit it and drew the tobacco until a thin grey spiral of smoke rose around him.

"Well... we'll see lass... won't we?"

Tom grabbed her hand beneath the table and squeezed it to reassure her again.

The young couple sat beside the fire and discussed what they should do next. It would not be easy to escape the scrutiny of Swarbrick's gang. They had to get a message to the Custom House at Lancaster, but that would take more than a day by horse. Before they did anything Tom had to find his superior officer, the Revenue agent, and inform him of the situation. The problem was, he was based at Piel, which meant travelling back towards Rampside... and the smugglers. They might never make it to Piel, but if they split up, then maybe they would have a chance.

It was decided that they would go to Mote Farm, where Tom's brother lived. Tom needed a fresh horse, since his was still in the yard of the Concle Inn, probably claimed in compensation by Swarbrick for losing his prisoners. Dolly was to make her way back to Rampside along the coast and hide until low tide so that she could cross the sands to Piel Island, where the Revenue agent stayed. They would need reinforcements and Tom would see to that. He would ride through night and day to Lancaster, covering the miles on horseback.

At daybreak Tom slipped out of the house and saddled the horse. The way was long and dangerous; he was determined to take a risk and travel across the sands to Lancaster. He had done it before, with a guide, but he believed he could remember the way. It would be too dangerous to appoint a guide this time; Swarbrick would hear about it and give chase. He knew the sands were treacherous and ever shifting, but this was the only way to shorten his journey and return to Dolly quickly.

It was barely light. A thin greyness wisped its tendrils across the bay, snatching at the weak sunlight, forcing its way through the clouds. Tom rode on across the bubbling sand, the horse unsure of the ground and faltering. A dense blanket of mist descended, wrapping Tom in a damp, clammy cloak. He could see neither ahead nor behind, his vision totally obscured by the impenetrable fog. The horse grew nervous and he gave an anxious whinny. Tom patted his neck, whispering to calm him. Beneath the horse's feet, waves lapped and bubbled up from under the sand.

The horse reared and fought against the rising tide, shaking Tom from his back like an annoying insect. He reared again, jumped and raced into the mist, leaving Tom stranded and rolling in the wet sand. He rose to his feet and looked round in panic, staggering, his feet being sucked into the sand with each frenzied step he took. Within mere minutes he was knee deep in cloying, heavy mud. He knew his end had come. He would perish here on the sands, so close to Dolly yet so far and never to see her more.

CHAPTER 8

TIME LAPSE

Nate stood on the mound looking across the sands. Wind blew sand and rain over the open landscape, blasting the contours of the coast, over time moulding and changing its features. The sky met the sea in the distance, spreading a grey blanket that obscured the horizon. He pondered about the quest and still found it hard to comprehend. He had a map to discover; where that could be in this hostile place he could not imagine. If the hoard had been buried close he must be able to find it. The sword was more difficult. It had been rescued but then lost again – how would this be resolved? Someone had taken it and had deliberately hidden it; this would be much harder to locate.

Aldingham Motte was a good vantage point for the quest, but how useful it would be was debatable. As he stared out to sea he could see a rider fighting his way across the inhospitable sands. A cloak of sea mist wrapped around the figure, obscuring him from view. The rain grew heavier and Nate strained to see the rider emerge from the mist. It cleared for seconds, revealing the horse rearing and the rider falling backwards on to the mud. Fingers of fog played with the figures and Nate jumped as the horse finally bolted and disappeared into the greyness. The rider then vanished from view too.

Nate ran to the next field and scrambled over the fence. He slipped and scrambled down the cliff side, sending stones and mud rattling down to the beach below. He caught his clothes on the brambles and his arms were scratched and bruised. He fell the last few feet, landing heavily on to the pebbles and shingle. Picking himself up, he ran down the beach towards the place where he had last seen the rider. The mist descended and swirled around the boy as he ran across the sands. Very quickly he was encased in dense, grey, damp fog, his heart hammered at his chest and his throat compressed with fear like a noose around his neck. He turned quickly this way and that, looking for a familiar feature to help him find his way. None was evident. His feet began to sink and squelch into the mud and water stole around his legs, making him panic further.

He pulled his foot out of the mud with a huge effort and fell sprawling across the fluid sands. He dragged himself along the ground, the water rising fast. A silhouette flickered and glimmered ahead of him, shrouded in an ethereal silver light. It moved closer and Nate stiffened with fear. A hand reached down and heaved him to his feet. The two connected and the grey world span around them. They were overcome with giddiness and nausea as they lost orientation and direction. Then... blackness.

Nate opened his eyes slowly. His head throbbed and small flashes of light ran back and forth across his vision. He blinked and rubbed them, slowly sitting up. He felt cold and damp, his clothes heavy with sand and grit. The greyness had dissipated, replaced by a pale, watercolour sky. He looked around to establish where he was. Astonishingly he was above the beach on the banking, facing out to sea again, as if he had never moved. He wondered whether he had dreamed it all and turned to stand up. He flinched suddenly as he saw another figure sprawled on the wet grass before him. So it hadn't been a dream! The person on the beach... who had grabbed his hand, pulling him to safety, was there in front of him – real flesh and blood.

Almost telepathically the figure stirred as though he knew he was being stared at. The fellow sat up, brushing sand from his clothes. He stopped suddenly, as soon as he caught sight of Nate. Both boys stared at each other, but neither spoke. They inspected each other in disbelief.

"Who... what ... " began Nate.

"What strange apparel thou dost wear, lad," interrupted the tall youth.

"Me? Strange? What about you?" retorted Nate.

The youth merely stared hard, considering the boy before him. He shrugged and continued to dust down his cloak. He wore the thick woollen cloak over a waistcoat, breeches and shirt. His legs were encased in leather top boots and he bent to pick up a tricorn hat, which he proceeded to brush with his hand. He glanced at Nate as he stood up, his eyes travelling over his fedora, Doc Marten boots, jeans and waterproof jacket. He looked puzzled, but did not say anything.

"Who are you?" asked Nate bluntly.

"I am the Revenue officer for this coast, Tom Rallison," he said, growing a few inches taller with pride. "And who be thee?"

"I live at Roose and I'm an archaeologist," said Nate, bristling with similar pride.

"I know not what an arch… archil…"

"Archaeologist!" interjected Nate, smiling. "I dig up old pots, bones and stuff."

"Thou art a mudlark?" hissed Tom, "A scavenger. I trust thou art honest, lad?"

"Well, I dunno about mudlark, but I am honest. Cheek!"

"I mean no offence, lad… but 'tis an unusual occupation for a strong lad like thee. Hast thou no farm work or fishing to occupy thee?"

"I don't need to work, I live at home with my Mam and Dad and I still go to school. Anyway, you can't be a Revenue officer – you're too young… and while were on it, why are you dressed like a highwayman? 'You going to a fancy dress party or summat?"

It became apparent that they were not speaking the same language.

A gust of wind blew, driving sand across the beach. The movement awoke them from their torpor and both youths looked around. Tom started striding across the headland. Nate stood glued to the spot. As he gazed around the familiar landscape, he suddenly realised that it was not as familiar as he first thought. Tom was striding over the field towards Mote Farm, which looked different and rustic. A thin plume of smoke rose from the chimney and people were moving around the farmyard, making noise and working. Nate looked towards the road, but instead of the coastal road there was a dirt track leading away from the farm towards the direction of Gleaston. He spun round, to look back at the sea and the horizon, to find familiar landmarks.

He could no longer see Heysham Nuclear Power Station, or evidence of the towns of Morecambe and Blackpool... not even the famous Tower was visible. He strained to see towards Rampside and Piel and was shocked to see the former was an island; its familiar causeway had disappeared. No bungalows or houses remained, no road and even the Motte looked odd. It was further away from the cliff edge and covered in brambles and plants.

He was shocked to the point of being sick. Tom turned to see him throwing up on the grass.

"What ails thee, lad?" he cried.

Nate rested his hands on his knees and bent low. He shook himself and stood up, rubbing his head as he did so. Tom had reached him and looked on in concern.

"Come, I'll take thee to my brother's home, 'tis just over yonder," he said, waving an arm towards the farm.

Nate did not object. He followed the strange youth, feeling conspicuous sporting his bright blue waterproof jacket. He removed it and rolled it up, tucking it under the hedge, to retrieve later. He felt at least his black checked, fleeced shirt was less at odds and he hoped he could blend in better. Thoughts raced through his head, he could make no sense of things. His mind told him that he was in a different time zone, but he could not accept it. How this could have happened he could not explain, but more importantly, why had it happened? This was scarier than when time stood still in the field at Gleaston.

They reached the muddy farmyard and the farm hands working in the outbuildings looked at him curiously as he followed Tom into the house. It was here that the sharpest difference struck him. An open fire, with a pot suspended above it, warmed and partially lit the dim kitchen. The smell of soup rose from the black pot and he realised how long it was since he had eaten. A rough wooden table filled the small room surrounded by roughly hewn benches and two Windsor chairs stood beside the fire separated by a rag rug, the only floor covering visible. There did not appear to be much furniture – apart from a dresser in the corner. A young woman in a long dress covered by an apron was stoking the fire. She replaced the poker on the hearth and wiped her hands on the apron.

"Tom!" she exclaimed. "Thou art back swiftly?"

"Aye! I fell into danger across the sands. The horse bolted and I was left to fettle for myself until this young lad came to my rescue."

The girl, whose name was Mary, produced a loaf of gritty – looking bread, two wooden bowls full of a thick vegetable soup and two cups of ale. Nate ate mindlessly. The day could not become much stranger and who knew how long he was going to be stuck here in… whatever year this was!

The day passed and Tom shared his story of smugglers and escape. He spoke fondly of Dolly and how he had failed to reach the Customs at Lancaster.

Nate shared nothing of his quest; he felt until he knew more it would not be safe to do so. He explained he came from a far distant time, but was not sure how much they understood this.

Days melted into weeks. Nate fell into gloom, wondering if he would ever see his family again. Tom and Dolly, whom he had met the same day he had arrived in the past, both tried to comfort him and make him welcome. Dolly had turned back to Aldingham because Swarbrick's men were abroad at Goadsbarrow and she dared not pass them.

Nate borrowed some of Tom's brother Jack's clothes, to blend in a little better. He felt uncomfortable in the rough fabrics and insisted on retaining his own hat, T-shirt, boxer shorts and boots, which Tom had found hilarious. He soon became grubby and smelly, as he quickly discovered that clothes washing and bathing were not high on the agenda in 1750. Eventually he grew used to the aroma and made sure he washed well each day with the foul-smelling piece of homemade soap that Mary had given him on request. The food, too, took an immense effort to get used to. The variety was limited and the meat they had tasted differently to that at home. The diet included fish and shellfish, taken from the sands below the farm, and they did have fresh eggs from the many hens running around the yard. However, his stomach was delicate and unused to the diet and he suffered with griping pains for the first few days.

Tom was anxious to bring his smugglers to book, and one evening as they sat around the crackling log fire, the women sewing by candlelight, he began speaking.

"I must yet apprehend these villains and find the treasure they so keenly seek."

Nate nearly choked on the ale he was drinking.

"What? Treasure?" he spluttered.

"Aye lad, treasure and 'tis my chart they crave."

Nate thought all his birthdays had come at once.

"A map? Do you mean a map?" he cried excitedly.

"Of course, 'twas how I stumbled upon their evil trade. It led me to their cache in the tunnel. And right beside the Customs House at Piel it was! The boldness of them, hiding their booty beneath the noses of the Excise men."

"This map – do you still have it, Tom?"

"Aye, I keep it in my wes'cot, here," he said, patting his chest.

"May I see it?" begged Nate.

"You may… why art thou so interested in it?"

"Because… because we may have a connection… because it may be the key to why I am here in your time… because I have treasure to find in my time."

Tom considered this for a moment and then answered.

"I think it's time we both shared what we know."

Nate nodded and told the young man all he knew, about Chris, the skull and the lost treasure.

"So thou think 'tis likely to be one and the same treasure we both seek?" Tom asked.

"I do!" replied Nate simply.

Tom took out the map and unfolded it, smoothing it out on the table. He explained that he had found the map at the Custom House on Piel, not long after he had arrived. It was old and showed tunnels and pathways all over the district, many of them leading to the abbey. At first he had not taken much notice of it, but then he had seen the tangle of tunnels and their proximity to the inn. He knew that the smugglers were always just one step ahead of the Excise officers and wondered if they too knew of these tunnels. He had soon discovered the answer, coming across them one dark night and finding a huge cache of contraband. The contraband was not the least of it, there was a small collection of golden artefacts too, strange and old. He was shocked to see them because some were religious in nature, bejewelled and gaudy; something that these days were not approved of, they were of the Roman religion. The more he spoke, the surer Nate was that this was the map which Chris had mentioned.

Tom and Nate decided to explore the tunnels as soon as day broke. They knew they would have to be careful as Swarbrick's gang were still out for their blood, but the Excise men had been finally alerted to the gang's exploits and they were now in hiding. Tom was back to his duties and he knew that to solve the problem once and for all would be to locate the treasure and expose the many hiding places of the smugglers.

Dolly had listened quietly. She suddenly broke her silence.

"I will come too," she said.

"That thou shalt not!" Tom exclaimed. "'Twill be too dangerous for a girl!"

Nate sniggered.

"Dangerous! I care not. I want these villains out of my father's life and I will be part of this, as I have been all along," she asserted firmly.

Tom opened his mouth to protest, but Nate interrupted swiftly.

"Come on, Tom! She's got a point and she's been in danger before … we'll be with her!"

"'Tis not seemly! She is but a woman."

Nate winced; he wouldn't get away with that attitude in the present. Dolly stood up, drawing herself to her full height, and exclaimed, "And thou art only a man… and I will go with thee!"

And so she did.

Chapter 9

Rampside

It was strange to see the Concle again, Dolly had not been back since the night Tom had rescued her. Dawn was just breaking and the strange half-light cast an ethereal glow. They crept along the edge of the beach and pushed the small rowing boat out into the gently lapping waves. Tom and Nate took an oar each and they rowed past Roa Island and on to Piel. They beached the boat on the shoreline and ran quickly up to the castle. It had fallen into disrepair, but Nate was surprised to see that more existed in this time than his own. The east tower in his time had slipped some way down the hill and on to the beach, yet here it was still in place.

They crouched down behind the castle wall and opened the map again. They looked for the entrance to the tunnel and where it branched off. Tom whispered, "We must climb down this shaft first and from there we can move onward. I reckon this tunnel connects with others. I took the tunnel at the far side of the island, but it did only lead to a small cave where the cache was hid."

He revealed a rotting grille hidden among the undergrowth, covering a deep hole. Somebody had tied a rope to one of the bars and it dangled far below, the end vanishing into darkness.

Nate whistled. "How are we gonna get down without light, we won't be able to see?"

"What is it?" asked Dolly, peering over the edge.

"I know this... it's what they call an oubliette – for prisoners and such."

They both accepted Nate's explanation and asked no further questions. They seemed happy that such a place should be reserved for prisoners.

Tom had a bag with him and he placed it on the floor and took a tallow candle from inside.

"We can use these, but sparingly."

He replaced the candle and they prepared to lower themselves into the shaft. Nate was lowered down first, at Tom's insistence, so he could catch Dolly when it was her turn. It wasn't quite as dark as it looked at the bottom, but Nate couldn't fathom where there would be an exit from the shaft. He waited for Dolly to land and he looked upwards to catch her. He could see her voluminous skirts and petticoats flapping around her legs and suddenly a leather shoe hit him squarely in the face. Before he could recover, Dolly let go of the rope and she landed on top of him. They fell in a crumpled heap and could not help but laugh.

Minutes later Tom jumped from the end of the rope and helped Dolly up. They collected themselves and Tom took out the candle. He lit it with a tinder box which he took from his pocket.

The candle illuminated the bottom of the shaft with a weak yellow light. They looked around the roughly hewn walls and were unable at first to find an opening. Nate felt around the walls with the palms of his hands, just as he had seen in films, hoping to discover a lever or a gap revealing a tunnel. Tom joined him, both of them absorbed in what they were doing. Tom almost dropped the candle when he turned around to speak to Dolly. She was gone! Both boys called her name, in fear. What had happened to her in such a confined space?

Then, almost as quickly as she had disappeared; she returned. She was grinning from ear to ear. She seemed to step from nowhere.

"Look, there is a gap behind this wall – it leads to a tunnel," she explained excitedly.

"Where? I can't see one!" exclaimed Nate, in disbelief.

Dolly grabbed his hand and pulled him to the wall opposite. She felt along the edge where the two walls met and vanished behind. There was a false wall at one end, with a narrow gap, large enough to slip behind, which led to another wall parallel to the original wall in the shaft, again with a small gap. So, to the naked eye it could not be seen.

"Aw! It's like an optical illusion!" said Nate. "No way was this a dungeon – the prisoners would have escaped."

"Aye, but what a great deception! The monks were clever, 'twould look like a dungeon and would not arouse suspicion – not a soul would guess it was a tunnel."

The three friends slipped behind the wall and into the passage which seemed to lead downwards. They lit a second candle and walked carefully onwards.

The way was dark, rocky and narrow in parts. The further they travelled the darker and steeper it became.

They were all silent, partly from the deep concentration they needed to find their way and partly because they were unsure of what… or who lay ahead. The tunnel was quiet and became warmer the deeper they went. After a while they could make out a strange rushing sound, and little taps or knocks above them. At first they could not understand what it was and then Nate suddenly had a brainwave.

"Oh my God! I know what that is! It's the sea! We're under the bloody sea! It's the water and the rocks moving above us!"

"We will drown and ne'er be found!" cried Dolly, panic stricken.

"No, we won't! This tunnel has been here for… for centuries and it's not even wet down here!" retorted Nate.

"I am sure we are safe, Dolly, as Nate says… the tunnel has been here many a long year," added Tom kindly.

They continued on and the tunnel levelled out. They came to a fork and they moved into an area with huge wooden supports appearing at intervals along the way. It widened for a while and the sandy floor showed signs of footprints here and there were scattered tools and the detritus of labour. It was obvious that they had strayed into old mine workings, and from the appearance of them they had not been used for many years.

"I did hear tell that the old monks had labourers who mined the land for iron. 'Tis likely that these are their workings," offered Tom thoughtfully.

"Wow! So that's how the tunnel stories began! The miners must've dug it out for the monks. It can't go that far though – they only had hand picks…" Nate said.

"And, pray, what else would a miner have but hand picks?" asked Tom.

"Machinery, drills!" Nate answered. "But… you won't have seen anything like that yet… trust me – you wouldn't believe it!"

"Aye, there is much thou sayest that I cannot believe or even understand!" laughed Tom.

Dolly sank to the floor, wearied from the journey. She removed her shoe and tipped out the sand and small stones which had accumulated there.

"I cannot walk a step further. I must take water, I am parched quite dry!" she sighed.

The boys sank to the floor gladly. Tom blew out one of the candles and took off the leather costrel he was carrying around his waist. They each took a drink and soon felt much better. They took out the map once more and tried to locate their whereabouts. The maze of tunnels was confusing once they were past the undersea section. However, they could see there was a way forward and hoped they were still going in the right direction, though being this deep underground it was hard to tell. When they had rested they collected their belongings and moved on. The tunnels narrowed and widened and at times were hard to move through. On more than one occasion they had to double back retracing their steps because the way was a dead end or blocked by fallen rock.

They had been walking for what seemed an age when they noticed ahead of them a pale yellow light, flickering and fading. They jumped back behind a rocky outcrop and crouched, whispering hurriedly.

"What is it? It could be your smugglers, Tom?" prompted Nate.

"It may be the daylight?" ventured Dolly optimistically.

"I think not, it looks like lanterns or candlelight to me," Tom shook his head. "We cannot go back, but we must take care moving forward. I will go towards the light and see what dangers are ahead. Wait here with Dolly, Nate, and watch for my signal. Blow out the candles."

He spoke with such authority that Nate did as he was told. He and Dolly watched Tom creep down the tunnel towards the light. He kept close to the wall and then slowly disappeared from view. The atmosphere was tense as they crouched, quietly waiting for Tom to return. The pair shot anxious glances at each other, both worried and concerned for their friend's safe-keeping.

Their thoughts were shattered by Tom's sudden reappearance. He slid along the ground next to them, sending stones and dirt in every direction.

"'Tis them! Swarbrick and his gang, just ahead. They have much booty and contraband," he whispered agitatedly.

"Well, you can't nick 'em now, Tom! It's too dangerous and we don't know another way out!" hissed Nate.

Tom raised his eyebrows, "I conjecture that 'nick' means apprehend?"

Nate grinned and nodded.

"I am not so foolhardy as to risk Dolly's and thy safety for a cache of tobacco and rum... but I will return, as is my duty, later. Meanwhile, we needs must travel around them without being seen; 'twill be difficult, but if we stay together we will succeed."

The three of them crept down the passage the same way Tom had. As they turned the corner, the path fell away into a cavern where the smugglers were moving their plunder. On the far side of the poorly lit cave was another tunnel; the smugglers were carrying barrels and boxes into the cave. There were half a dozen of these ruffians, directed by Swarbrick who sat atop a barrel smoking a clay pipe and calling out gruff instructions.

Not for the first time since he had been in the eighteenth century Nate felt afraid. The talk of smugglers had seemed exciting before, but now, confronted with real, brutal men armed with knives and pistols, it did not seem so anymore.

On the right, nearest to Swarbrick, another passage entrance revealed itself. Tom signalled silently to them to follow. He crawled between rocks and boxes behind Swarbrick, towards the opening. The other two followed close behind, Dolly in between the boys. The opening was slightly behind him and the three would have to pass extremely close to escape down the other passage. Tom led them within a few feet of Swarbrick and they halted at the tunnel mouth. Tom went first, watching for the other men and making sure nobody was looking his way. He slipped into the tunnel and disappeared into the darkness. Nate was moist with sweat, he could hardly breathe he was so tense. Dolly was next and she looked as terrified as he felt. She lifted her skirts and made a run for the tunnel. She too vanished into shadows. It was his turn now. He froze as Swarbrick stood up and stretched. The man still had his back to him, but he was speaking to another smuggler who was now facing in his direction. His stomach churned and he wanted to run, but knew he would need to gauge his movements exactly to avoid being caught.

The two men were laughing and talking and Nate slowly moved towards the entrance. As he stretched, ready to run, a cry went up from the smuggler facing him. Nate stopped for a second and then ran for all he was worth into the tunnel. He crashed into Dolly, knocking her over. The two boys pulled her swiftly to her feet and dragged her headlong into the tunnel. They had no candlelight and could hardly see where they were going, but the noise of the pursuing smugglers urged them on. Dolly screamed as one of the men pulled her hair and tried to drag her back. Tom launched himself at the man and knocked him over, rolling him into the tunnel wall. The man lay inert on the floor and they ran on. Two more men scrambled towards them, but they were quicker and nimbler and raced onward into the darkness. Nate, who had run ahead, rolled a large rock into their path, to buy them a little time.

They finally reached a fork in the tunnel and sped along the left-hand side. They ran until their chests felt they would burst, but eventually, could hear their pursuers no longer.

They collapsed in the dark and all that could be heard was their heavy panting and an occasional sob from Dolly. The heat was oppressive and all felt in need of a drink. They silently supped from the flask.

"We are safe now!" said Tom "We must find our way out of here."

"And how do you suggest we do that? I can't remember which way to go from the map can you?" contradicted Nate.

"And we cannot go the way we came… how will we get home?" pleaded Dolly.

Tom was crestfallen. He had no answers and he now had to break the news that he had dropped the map and had no directions to offer at all.

He decided to bluff and limit their panic.

"I know this is the way, I recall the direction – 'tis straight forward from here to the outside."

He stood and relit the candle from his bag. The tunnel ahead was very narrow. They trudged their way along, the width narrowing as they went. The shaft became very oppressive and Nate began to feel claustrophobic. Soon they were bent double and within minutes the height of the tunnel had dropped so much that they were crawling on hands and knees.

"I like this not!" whimpered Dolly.

"That's two of us then," added Nate "Hey Tom! You sure this is the way?"

Tom did not answer. The candle went out and they were plunged into darkness again. They heard a rattling of stones and a thud, followed by a string of eighteenth-century curses.

Dolly squealed, as she too slipped down the sudden slope in the tunnel and landed heavily on top of Tom. Nate followed quickly and winded the other two.

When they had collected themselves Tom lit the candle and they could gain a better view of their location.

The tunnel had dropped some feet down and had opened up into an extinct mine working. It was at least encouraging that there was evidence that miners had been this way. They ate some bread and cheese which Tom had in his bag and finished the remainder of the water; then moved towards the only exit and followed it upwards. The temperature began to change, becoming a bit fresher and cooler. There was little room to manoeuvre and they walked in single file. The tunnel smelt dank and as they carried on upwards trickles of water ran down the walls. Soon they could feel a definite breeze on their faces and their steps quickened. The tunnel levelled off again and they found they were walking in little puddles of muddy water. The darkness was less dense and they passed a break in the wall. The hole led them towards daylight, so they stepped from their path and walked into the new tunnel.

This was lined with red sandstone bricks and the floor was clay and very wet. It was obvious that this was no mine tunnel but something more finely engineered. As they walked along, a shaft of light shone down, just ahead.

They were now walking bent over because the height had reduced. They came to rest beneath a grille, similar to the one at the castle. Voices could be heard above.

They sounded like children. But they could take no risks and remained silent.

As the voices got clearer Nate looked puzzled. One voice seemed familiar.

"Something strange happened to us last night… there were weird creatures… and the monk… at our houses," it said.

"It's my sister! It's Rebecca!" he hissed. "We are in my time! I'm BACK!"

The other two looked incredulously at him.

"I'll shout her… she'll help us!" he jumped up, banging his head on the tunnel roof.

A shadow fell across the grille. A figure came into view. He was dressed in a long white robe, with a black scapula over the top, tied with a rope belt.

Nate nearly fainted with shock. Tom and Dolly stood frozen with fear.

The monk smiled and raised a hand in benediction. He then placed a long index finger over his lips to silence them and shook his head.

He gestured them to continue along the tunnel.

They did so without question.

Tears prickled the back of Nate's eyes, his comprehension confounded by this last turn. He knew where they were alright, they had reached the abbey! But why would a monk… in his own time… stop him from shouting Rebecca? Was he ever going to get out of this predicament?

They carried on until the culvert opened out into daylight. They were at the foot of Abbot's Wood and it was sunny and warm. They looked a complete mess. Muddy, dishevelled and weary, they flopped on to the banking, under the trees. Nate didn't know quite how to tell his companions that they were now in the twenty-first century. But for now they would rest and work out what to do next.

The warm sun made them drowsy and they fell asleep on the soft grass. When they awoke an hour had passed, but they felt much better. Nate cleared his throat and struggled to think what to do. Tom broke the silence instinctively.

"So, what dost thou think we should do now? For we are in thy time, I suspect?"

Dolly turned sharply when he spoke and shock spread across her face. She had never really believed that Nate was from a different time to her and Tom, and suggesting that they had travelled to the future was too much to bear. Panic rose in her chest and constricted her breathing, her eyes welled with tears and she began to sob. Tom put his arm around her and the three of them sat in silence.

Eventually Nate spoke.

"I've got an idea... but I don't know if it will work..."

"Speak, for we need to consider some remedy to this situation," answered Tom, his voice hollow.

"Well... you have to be brave... I know it's scary... I felt the same in your time. You're gonna see things which will be more than you can imagine and I guess you will be frightened, but trust me, you'll be safe – promise!" Nate reassured them.

He jumped to his feet and walked behind the trees, leaving the two to come to terms with the situation. He delved into his pocket, where his Nokia mobile had been since he had been on the headland at Aldingham… weeks ago. He took it out and prayed that it had held its charge since he had turned it off the day he reached the eighteenth century. He held his breath as he watched it light up. He was relieved and worried all in the same moment. Now to make the call – but could he rely on Tom and Dolly to play their parts? The mobile rang and someone responded. A short conversation ensued and Nate smiled and turned the phone off again.

He warned the two young people not to fear what they saw, and to do as he did and keep conversation to a bare minimum. He led them through the woods and down the steps, across the road to the Abbey Mill. Luckily not many people were about so they could keep a low profile. Within minutes an old, battered white Ford Fiesta appeared over the hill, trance music booming through the open windows. It screeched to a halt next to them. Dolly looked ready to faint and even Tom was visibly shaken. Rob was at the wheel and he leaned over and yelled at them to get in. Nate bundled them into the back seat and kept his fingers crossed that they wouldn't say much. He had no need to worry, both were too terrified to even move.

"You are seriously weird! What do you wanna do all this re-enactment stuff for?" he laughed.

"It's to help people get the idea of the past," lied Nate.

"All of you going then?" he said nodding to the others.

"Er yeah! They're with me," said Nate. "Did ya get the Maccies?"

"Doh! What do you think this is?" Rob said, lifting two brown bags from the well of the front seat as Nate got in. "And watch the drinks... don't knock 'em over!" he instructed.

Nate kept them with him; he did not want to overburden Tom and Dolly too much with strange things. They sped off towards Yarlside at an alarming rate of knots, Rob keeping up speed to the beat of the music. A small whimper escaped from Dolly's mouth. He glanced in the rear-view mirror at the two in the back.

"You're all freaks! And do you have to look so filthy? I'm sure they had soap in the eighteenth century!" he chuckled.

"I wouldn't bet on it Rob! But you wouldn't know!"

"Anyway, you owe me for the McDonald's and my petrol," Rob insisted. "'You back tomorrow? Mum was asking... she said you've gotta tidy your room before school on Monday."

Nate was surprised. They hadn't missed him? He had been away weeks... but Rob was talking as though he had seen him yesterday.

"What day is it today?" He laughed nervously.

"Plonker! It's Thursday... you dim or what?" retorted Rob.

"I forgot... it seems centuries since I was home," he quipped, laughing inwardly at his joke.

"No, you've only been camping since Monday – but Mum wants you back Saturday," added Rob with authority.

The car drew to a halt at the car park next to the Concle. Nate got out and grabbed the bags of food and the drinks. The two reluctant passengers scrambled out of the back seat and stood on the gravel. Dolly dropped a small curtsey in thanks for the end of the journey and Rob shook his head in disbelief.

"Freaks!" he muttered as he pulled away and sped off down the road back to Barrow.

They followed Nate across the car park, past the Concle towards the beach. Dolly lingered, unable to comprehend how different her home now looked. They flopped silently on to the beach bank. Nate handed out the fast food packets and placed them into his companion's hands. They both looked at it, unable to identify it as food.

"Eat!" commanded Nate, "It's good… its bread and meat… and the thin things are fries… you know, potatoes!"

Silence.

"Go on, you've gotta keep your strength up!" he urged.

They peered closely at the burgers and Tom lifted the bun to expose the burger. He stabbed it with his finger and licked the ketchup. He winced and shuddered. Dolly sniffed the fries and gingerly took one in her fingers, raising it to her lips. She began eating. They slowly ate the food, grimacing and glancing at each other.

"Well? Do you like it then?" asked Nate anxiously.

"'Tis like no meat I have ever tasted. What creature does this come from?" questioned Tom.

"Aye! And this bread tastes like nought I have eaten...'tis limp and... urgh!" added Dolly with a shudder.

When it came to the coke this was slightly more successful. There was some difficulty getting them to use a straw, but once they dispensed with that and drank from the open cup they managed well.

"This ale doth tingle on the tongue! It doth taste most sweet," giggled Dolly.

"Aye, 'tis strong and sweet to be sure, but it doth quench a thirst I declare!" rejoined Tom.

When they had done Nate collected the rubbish and placed it into a nearby bin.

They strolled along the beach and discussed what to do next. Nate suggested they try to get back to Piel and into the tunnel again – after all it was through that tunnel that they had travelled to the future. They couldn't risk going in the ferry dressed as they were and they had no modern money. They decided to bide their time until the tide turned and they would walk across. However, the tide would not turn in quite the way they had hoped.

CHAPTER 10

THE BERSERKER AD 650

The wind swept into the cove sending sand and debris hurtling across the beach, into the dunes. The power of the gale forced them to huddle closer behind the wreck, pulling their clothes tight about them for protection. Grains of sand spat and scratched at their skin and their hair tangled and matted in the wind. As they protected their eyes from the smarting bombardment the cloud of sand spun into a whirlpool gaining momentum and power. The drag of the airstream became more powerful and pulled them towards the eye of the storm. They tumbled and fell towards the phenomenon, whirling and rotating, until they could not tell beach from sky. Giddiness overcame them and they were disorientated, Dolly felt sick, and just as she could stand it no more they came to a halt, crashing into each other, like wreckage after a storm.

Before any of them could speak, a bright light filled the horizon, crashing waves subsiding, grey clouds melting into blue and a warm sun filtered into the clear sky. The friends froze, a chill running through their bodies even though it was a warm day. Out at sea, passing Piel Island a boat glided easily through the waves towards them.

"What is it?" gasped Dolly. "I've never seen a boat like that before."

Tom peered at the vessel, shaking his head in disbelief.

"For God's sake!" cried Nate excitedly. "It's a longship! A bloody Viking longship! What's going on?"

The longship sliced through the water like a keenly honed knife and was followed by two more. The rhythm of the oars was hypnotising and the sheer speed with which the boats drew near was terrifying. At the prow of the first ship stood a wild, red-haired Norseman, alert and as fierce as the painted dragon on the prow of his ship. The ships slid to shore, scattering the shingle as they slowed to a stop. The Viking leapt into the air raising his sword high above him, his war cry curdling the blood in the young people's veins. He landed heavily on the sand, screaming his battle-cry again and running towards the headland, his swordsmen crowding behind him. The noise of the men's cries split the tranquillity of the day and as they gathered, some armed with axes, some with spears or swords and many with more than one weapon, the youngsters shrank into the dunes hoping to be overlooked.

They had not seen on the headland a small force of local warriors, who were now racing to meet the Viking raiders. Behind them a beacon fire had been lit and its thin, wiry plume of smoke wove its way into the air, stitching the blue sky with grey. The friends pressed their bodies flat to the base of the sandhill and hardly dared breathe for fear of discovery. They had no need to worry – the Vikings had seen their quarry and ran rapidly towards the warriors, whooping and leaping joyously, impervious to the danger of battle. The noise was terrifying and ear-splitting. Metal clashed against metal, weapons hissed through the air, screams of agony met cries of triumph and victory. Bodies crashed heavily into each other, bones and skulls cracked and split, men fell to the ground never to arise again.

The gang watched in awe from their hide. Although they had endured some dangerous and scary adventures together, nothing compared to this. Dolly was shaking with fear and even the boys were ashen faced.

"I can't believe this… how are we here?" whispered Nate.

"I know not! 'Tis foul magic of some devising!" answered Tom, horror-struck by the carnage before them.

It seemed ages before the battle ceased and the companions fell silent, unable to tear away their gaze from the dreadful scene. Finally, the party of warriors from the headland were so diminished after their brave struggle that the remaining men fled across the bloodied beach. The tall, red-haired Viking who had first leapt from the dragon ship gave chase, followed by a few of his number. Two men were seized and were dispatched cleanly. A few of the others escaped over the rise towards the small church beyond. The Viking raiders collected the weapons which had fallen from both sides and slung their haul into the ships. They regrouped, now much calmer, and began marching towards the small hamlet and the church over the fields. The companions crawled along the back of the sand dunes to watch. They crept silently along the edge of the dunes, keeping well out of sight.

In a split second the friends were wrenched from their hiding place by rough, strong hands. As they struggled and screamed, flailing and fighting to be free, a rich laugh rang out across the beach. The band of raiders looked back and acknowledged the guttural words coming from the mouths of their strapping captors. Dolly was slung easily over a dark-haired warrior's shoulder as though she weighed no more than a feather. She wriggled and squealed, trying to break free. He paced ahead, catching up with the other raiders. The lads were half carried and half dragged along, until they too reached the raiding party. Each time they tried to escape they were smacked around the head with the powerful flat of the warriors' hands.

A conversation continued between the men, interspersed with harsh laughter. The three knew that their fate was the source of the amusement. As they reached the dip before the small village of Crivelton, screams arose from the huts. Women and children ran asunder, away from the raiders. As the warriors ran through the village, plundering and setting fire to the huts, more screams pierced the smoky air. Prisoners were taken and rounded up with the three friends, guarded by just a couple of Vikings brandishing sharp axes and swords. The children were crying and everyone was terrified. It became obvious they were to be taken as slaves. Nate had read about captives being taken from England to be sold in Ireland as slaves by the Norsemen.

The only men left in the village were those too old or infirm to fight and these were ignored and pushed away. Those who did attempt to fight were slaughtered on the spot without hesitation.

The village was silent. Unexpectedly, the silence was split by the resonant peal of the church bell. Monks rang the alarm, alerting the surrounding area to the danger. The prisoners were dragged towards the small wooden church and left near a tree, guarded still.

Suddenly a small party of local Saxons from a settlement east of Crivelton raced into the village wielding fierce weapons, filling the air with bloodcurdling cries. The Saxons had responded to the beacon fire warning of the danger. The tall, red-haired chief rallied his berserkers to his side and a great battle ensued. The youngsters could hardly bear to watch. Brutal fighting on both sides took its toll, heavy clashes of steel followed by the dull thuds of bodies falling to the ground. The cruel noise of battle filled the dusk, showing no sign of abating. Finally, after what seemed like hours, the wooden church was on fire and the monks lay dead, alongside their Saxon kinsmen. Few Saxons remained standing and the Norsemen were assured their victory until, swiftly and unexpectedly, a boy of no more than fourteen leapt from behind a burning hut swinging a war axe half his height in length.

He took Red Hair by surprise, smashing the long sword from his hand, sending it spinning through the air, landing like a javelin in the earth, vibrating with the energy from the blow. With a second blow he hit him fair in the chest, felling him like a pine tree. The Vikings rounded on the lad, grabbing and slashing at him with their swords. One blade glanced off his shoulder and he stumbled momentarily, but he was nimble and managed to twist and squirm free. His fellow warriors banded together to allow him to escape. The lad ran for his life, the older warriors fought valiantly, finally retreating across the field towards the coast and away from the bloody Battle of Crivelton.

Nate thought he was going to be sick. Dolly was. Tom was paralysed with shock and all around them children and women cried and murmured with fear. The warriors took up their leader's body and placed his sword in his hands across his chest. They dug a shallow pit and lay his body and sword within. Across his chest they positioned a wooden shield and added smaller grave goods to go with him to Valhalla, the drinking hall of Odin and his heroes. Not for him a burning ship burial; the dragon ship was needed. Soberly they piled earth on top of him, raising a mound above him, which in the following years would become part of the landscape.

The wind rose blowing leaves and ash around, becoming a whirlpool of energy. Their fellow captors faded and flickered like an old movie. The Norsemen and the carnage they had wrought diminished like a bad memory. They were back to where they had started and were safe once more.

Nobody spoke. It was all too much to take in. Nate broke the silence.

"All that killing…"

Dolly screwed up her eyes and shuddered.

"Aye! Such killing!" responded Tom. "I've seen violence in my time, I have witnessed hangings at Lancaster – 'tis nought to compare with those… devils!"

"But why, pray, did we have to see such torment?" asked Dolly.

Silence.

Each thought their own thoughts.

Chapter 11

Revelations

"I know… I know what it is!" The light dawned on Nate. "It's the sword! It's *the* sword! The red-haired Viking! He's the one that stole it!"

"Nay! Think'st thou so?" replied Tom in astonishment. "That heathen devil – was the one who took the holy sword that slew St Oswald?"

"Well, why else were we treated to such a film show?"

"Film show?" Tom grimaced, unsure of what he meant.

"Oh!" Nate sighed in exasperation, "Never mind… er… you know, like a play, the theatre? You must have theatres in your time!"

"Aye that we do, though I have never been to such a place. 'Twould be costly. I did once see a circus… aye 'twas a grand…"

"Whatever!" retorted Nate impatiently. "What I'm getting at is – we saw the sword buried with him… we didn't get hurt… we were *supposed* to see it. Just like we *had* to meet on the beach, even though we are from a different time! Don't you see, it's another piece of the puzzle?"

It took seconds to allow the information to sink in fully. The three looked at each other, each with the same thought.

"We need to find where the Viking is buried." Nate shook his head. "But where will it be? It looks nothing like where we are now."

"Nay, ye are not thinking, Nate. We can surely recognise the place by the church?"

"S'pose it's a start... but I've no idea where the village is... and what if the church isn't in the same place?"

"Tis only one way to be sure, lads... we must repair to our church and see what places can be recognised!" Dolly jumped up briskly, brushed down her dress and pushed the strands of hair beneath her slightly grubby-looking cap.

The boys stood up and got their bearings. Night was drawing in, which did not leave much time. They scrambled up the banking and walked through the trees towards Rampside church, following the direction the raiding party had taken.

The quiet birdsong was in great contrast to the battle-cries that echoed in their memories, from the last time they had passed this way. The silhouette of the church stood proud against the pale pink sky of the emerging sunset. The rolling fields disguised any trace of Crivelton. Nate knew that there had been a village there many centuries ago, which had disappeared by his time. Nobody even knew where it had been. It seemed strange to imagine that the village had been rebuilt at all, after such dreadful destruction.

It was useless to look for the tree where they had been imprisoned. They had to look for a bump or mound. He remembered that the burial mound, though hastily constructed, had been on top of a small, natural drumlin which made it look bigger than it really was. The village had been in a small dip with the wooden church sitting slightly higher, along the rim of the small hill. Nate looked towards the church. The footpath ran into a hollow, a low-lying field and then up past the nineteenth century church. The church had replaced earlier chapels and it was said that it was the oldest place of worship in the area.

The sun was setting fast, gloom settling and mist beginning to rise like wraiths from the graveyard. From the field the church stood proud, perched on an egg-like mound. The hill looked less obvious with the large church crouching above it, but it had to be what they were looking for.

They ran towards the graveyard. Dolly grabbed Tom's arm. She was scared. They looked round in despair. Where would the Viking be? The graveyard had no burial mounds or bumps. Could it have been flattened or removed? They tried to orientate themselves, but there were no clues as to where he might lie.

"I believe we must go within yon chapel," suggested Tom.

"Better than stay in this bone yard…" whispered Dolly.

"I THINK YOU'RE RIGHT!" shouted Nate.

The others jumped from their skins.

"Sorry." Nate lowered his voice. "Didn't mean to scare you… but I think the mound is inside! The church has been built over it!"

They went to the door. Luckily it was still unlocked. There had been an open day earlier and the church had not yet been closed. The door creaked more loudly than they wished it to and they slipped inside and looked around. The final rays of the dying sun filtered through the windows. They crept around the nave walking towards the bell tower. Tom and Dolly were especially reverent, not really happy to be inside a church when no service was taking place. This church was not the one they knew in their own time, but it was still a holy place.

Nate moved quietly, hardly daring to breathe, until he came to the vestry. He lifted the latch and they went in.

Little revealed itself to them, but they wandered around looking for clues or indications of where the Viking might have been. There seemed to be no way down beneath the church and here and there were plaques and monuments, mostly from Victorian times. The carpet running down the nave of the church covered the floor and there was no way to look beneath. As they returned to the back of the church, they noticed the carpet runner was loose. Nate flipped it back to reveal a stone flag floor; disappointed, he replaced the carpet. The church kept its secret close, and hard as they tried they were unable to find a single clue to help them. Nate sank on to the nearest pew and sighed heavily.

Whatever were they supposed to do next? There was the treasure to find, Tom and Dolly needed to go back to their time and what was it all about anyway?

They all sat silently, becoming more sullen.

As they sat in the darkening church a noise disturbed the quiet. A scraping sound echoed around the church, but it was coming from outside. The three companions looked at each other and with a single movement jumped from their seats and moved towards the door. Tom pulled the heavy door open slowly and peered around the side. When he had assessed that it was safe to go out, he beckoned them to follow.

They slipped into the churchyard and discovered the source of the noise. At the back of the overgrown graveyard an elderly man was digging slowly but rhythmically.

"'Tis the gravedigger!" stated Tom with some authority.

"Do you think, Sherlock?" Nate sniggered.

Tom looked quizzically at him.

They watched for a minute and slowly the realisation dawned that they had shifted in time yet again. This man was dressed differently to all of them, he wore a grubby shirt with the sleeves rolled up, a buff-coloured waistcoat, a once red kerchief at his throat, shabby old trousers and scuffed leather boots laced with string. On the gravestone next to where he was digging was a folded jacket and perched on top of that a battered pork pie hat. He smoked a stubby clay pipe and had wispy white hair and whiskers framing his nut-brown, wrinkled face. Nate smirked to himself – he thought he looked like a garden gnome.

The man stretched and leaned on to his spade, breaking from his labour. He drew out a dirty rag from his pocket and wiped his brow, and drew on his pipe.

They moved closer, but he did not see them. As they stumbled over the uneven ground towards him he began digging again. He still did not see them. Eventually, they were so close they could have touched him, but he was oblivious to their presence.

"We aren't really here! He can't even see us!" gasped Nate incredulously.

"Aye! 'Tis true – he sees us not!" Tom shook his head, taking in yet another bizarre event which he could not explain.

"'Tis most peculiar!" Dolly agreed. "More strange magic methinks!"

Neither of the boys could disagree. Instead they watched this strange sideshow.

The old man was standing knee deep in the rectangular hole he had created. Again he rested and wiped the beads of sweat from his face, and something attracted his attention. He bobbed down into the grave so that all that could be seen of him was the arch of his back.

"Well, I'll be beggared!" he exclaimed in a gravelly voice.

He dug in the base of the grave and pulled at the soil-covered object. He brushed the soil gently from it, revealing the tip of a corroded lump of metal; he delved further and tugged hard. From over the boundary wall, about seven metres away, a younger man appeared. He was dressed similarly to the old chap but with a wide-brimmed hat.

"Aye up, father. I told thee t'wait on me!" he called.

"Nay, lad, I thowt I'd get a start on't… see – there's summat queer in't bottom o' t' hole. Tha can 'elp me get it out."

The young man bent, placing his large workman's hands on his knees, and peered into the grave. He straightened himself and took off his coat and hat, flinging them on to the ground beside him. He seized the shovel from his father, jumped into the hole next to him and began digging. The older man climbed out and knelt beside the hole.

"What dost tha make of it, Thomas? Can it be brought out in one piece?" he enquired.

The young man nodded and continued digging. Eventually he had cleared the object and was able to ease it out gently; as he stood up he held it in his hands and laid it carefully on the grass. Both men gazed at the object curiously. Thomas placed his foot on the tip and pressed the sword down to straighten it; it moved and a sickening crack snapped as the end of the brittle blade split.

"Well! I never did see owt like it in all my years as sexton in this church! It's an old sword, I reckon – as sure as my name's Jacob Helm!"

"Aye ! And there's other bits and pieces underneath, I'll bet on it!" rejoined Thomas, continuing to dig furiously.

"Tha'd best get on over t'rectory and tell minister to come over!"

The old man picked up his hat and coat and turned to leave. A sharp cry made him jump and turn around.

"Father! Look here!" cried his son.

He held a muddy lump in his hands and began brushing the earth from the object. A skull was revealed, looking like a leftover from Hallowe'en.

"Ha… this must be th'owner of the sword, I reckon," he sniggered. "An' look there's still some hair attached." He lifted a small lock of hair between his fingers and peered closely at his discovery.

"Looks like he was a red head as well!"

The three companions looked at each other and gasped. It was confirmed. The occupant of the grave was the Viking. How strange to see what he had become.

As the young man gloated over his find he was disturbed by the cawing of a raven. The swish of his large wings cut the air and the sleek, black bird swooped low, almost touching his head. The rapid movement surprised him and he lost his balance and fell backwards, the skull flying from his hands and landing on the grass with a thud.

A black feather floated down, spiralling in front of them, and the three off them felt a shudder run down their backs.

The Helms could be seen hurrying away from the grave towards the gate and a wispy, grey cloud coiled around the two retreating figures shrouding them in a dreary mantle. The colourless haze expanded and swallowed them up, smothering them in a clammy, dank blanket. The world began to spin and they lost their bearings completely. They whirled around as though they were on an invisible fairground ride, totally out of control and unable to stop. They felt nauseous and dizzy, finally coming to a halt, landing heavily on the ground.

It took some moments to recover as they surveyed their surroundings nervously. They were back at the shoreline where they had first encountered the Viking raid – was that only a few hours ago? Nate looked rapidly round and tried to locate familiar objects, hoping to see *his* Barrow in the distance, the Gas Terminal and other twenty-first century images. He was out of luck. It was easy to see they were back in the eighteenth century; the landscape was bereft of any sign of 21st century industry and Roa Island was still separated from the mainland. Tall ships with masts were docked in the harbour, the inn stood proud on the edge of the coast, and farmhands dressed like Tom were working the fields.

Nate sighed and put his head in his hands. He was quite unsure what to do to return to the present. Tom and Dolly were relieved, but concerned for their friend. After a short discussion they decided to try and find another entrance to the tunnel system under their feet. It was trial and error but they decided there must be a way back for Nate – and they *would* find it.

CHAPTER 12

SLIPPING THROUGH

Days had passed by again and Nate was seriously thinking he might never be able to return home. Tom had managed to track the Swarbrick gang to the cave they had passed through before, by another entrance near the coast at Conkin Bank. The Revenue men had caught some of them, but Swarbrick and the rest had escaped across the bay.

They discussed at length how Nate could get back and came to the conclusion that he should return to Furness Abbey. They were loath to journey through the labyrinth of tunnels again so Tom suggested they went above ground and find the exit from that end. They were no longer at risk from Swarbrick and his cronies so they confidently took the track across country to the Vale of Deadly Nightshade where the abbey lay.

Tom took two horses from his brother's farm and Dolly rode with him on the larger of the two. Nate followed behind, a little nervous, having had little experience of riding. The road they took was little more than two ruts in the ground where packhorses and carts had travelled. They passed close to St Michael's church… no evidence of the gravediggers in this time of course, and down the hill towards a tiny hamlet, which Nate supposed to be Roose. There were a few cottages and fields; he did recognise the Dungeon Lane and its farms on the way past, though the road was just a muddy track and all modern farm equipment had disappeared.

They rode on, passing a smithy where a blacksmith was busy at his anvil. Nate smiled to himself as he realised the "smithy" in his time was a fish and chip shop! Further up the lane was a large farmhouse outside some farm labourers were drinking ale. An old rickety sign creaked and rattled in the breeze. It was the Ship Inn and had been his Granddad's local pub in his time. It looked very different and hardly like a pub at all.

They wended their way onwards and he shivered involuntarily as the route wound its way above the river, for he knew this must be close to his home. No hint of the future was visible. No railway line, no houses and no real road. Weird!

They crossed a rough piece of open grazing land, dotted with sheep. This windswept grassy hill was high above the peninsula and he could see along to the coast. He stopped momentarily to look.

"'Tis Boulton's Common – the villagers may use this land to graze their animals and pay no rent..." Tom remarked.

Nate swallowed hard, a huge lump rising in his throat. His voice cracked with emotion. "And this is where I live in my time. My house will be built here years from now..."

Tom and Dolly looked sadly at him and beckoned him onwards. They continued on down past Park House Farm – again easily identified, and over Bow Bridge towards the abbey.

Through the trees they could see the sandstone glowing pink in the fading sunlight. They passed by the Abbey Mill and along the cobbled trackway, unchanged since medieval times. The railings and barriers to the abbey were not there and the building was brighter and sharper somehow. It was surrounded by trees and bushes and vegetation draped itself artfully over the masonry, dressing the abbey in a mantle of green.

They tethered the horses to a gnarled tree and sat on the grass, drinking in the spectacle of the abbey ruins. The remains were different – walls here and there which Nate would not have known in his time, no neat lawns and tidy trees, much wilder and in many ways more beautiful than the carefully manicured English Heritage version of the twenty-first century.

They drank from the leather flasks they had brought and rested for a while. They began to look for the tunnel they had travelled through and for the grate above it. They had not reckoned upon the tunnel being obscured by soil and overgrowth and it was difficult to locate. They heard a noise in the distance; it was coming from the cloister range. It sounded like… singing.

The hairs on the back of their necks stood up. The eerie half-light and the plaintive singing unnerved them. The haunting Gregorian chant filtered across the open cloister, beautiful and sad, but chilling considering that no monks had inhabited the abbey for at least two centuries. They stood petrified and yet fascinated. Dusk drew in and the final faded remnants of the day flickered and diminished like a guttering candle.

Within the chancel and Chapter House a pale yellow light emanated. A pale figure hovered effortlessly, moving through the cloister towards them. As he drew near his features became clearer and he smiled gently at them. The monk glimmered and flickered. He never spoke but gestured them to follow. Their fear had melted away and they were reassured by his placid presence. They walked through the passage to the undercroft and towards the kitchen. They found themselves at the abbot's house and below them was a partially concealed drainage tunnel. The monk gestured to Nate to enter the tunnel. Reluctantly he moved towards it. He stopped and ran back to Dolly and Tom. He could not be sure that he would see them again and he felt sad leaving them. He hugged them both and said a silent goodbye.

The monk smiled and said quietly, "Thy task cannot be fulfilled lest thou return to thy time and place. Thou wilt see thy companions more, so thy leave-taking need not be sad. Guard the knowledge of the sacred sword well and close, for there are those who would use it for ill. The sword which is known of in thy time is a mere shadow; 'tis not that which was found in the bone-yard at Rampside. The real sword lies concealed. It must be safe hid for the time when 'tis united with those other sacred relics, when they shall turn back the dark forces of time… one is nigh safe, but 'tis another's quest for now. Godspeed, my son, and trust thy friends will be out of harm's way."

He made the sign of blessing and turned slowly to walk away. Nate briefly looked at his friends… and then ducked to enter the tunnel. He reached the other end quickly, but could not resist looking back. All he could see was darkness.

He had slipped through time once more and as he emerged he could see the welcoming street lamps and hear the distant hum of traffic on Abbey Road. A dog walker passed the fence, and the familiar ring of a mobile phone incongruously broke the silence of the abbey. Home. He was home at last!

Chapter 13

A visit to the library

After the stress of the last few days, time travelling and not knowing what was going to happen next, a trip to the local library was a great relief. Usually he had to be forced to do any research and would not have chosen to be inside on a beautiful day like today. However, this was not a usual time; in fact, it was most unusual. True, it was exciting and amazing; but terrifying too. Each time he had crossed into the past he had been afraid that he might not be able to get home again. Tom and Dolly had been very understanding and had recovered from their brief interlude in the twenty-first century. He thought that their experience must have been even scarier than his, what with the change in landscape and the terrifying technology they had encountered. His experience was the reverse, it was a matter of losing the familiar places and objects, but because he knew something about the time he visited he could at least understand it. However, he did not relish being stuck there, as interesting as it was.

He went through the automatic doors and into the library. He glanced to the left and noticed a sign and some stone stairs leading to the upper floor. He was taken by surprise a little as he had never known the library to be open upstairs. The sign directed him to the Reference Library and he ran up the steps, to the top. He reached a wide landing, with two doors at either side. He looked in amazement at the double glass doors, which were open, revealing an emporium of artefacts and exhibits.

There were no visitors except for a young boy who was peering into a glass case. Nate browsed, looking at the exhibits – huge ships, apprentice models like those he had seen in the Dock Museum; row upon row of flint axes, apparently found at Biggar; a piece of stained glass from Furness Abbey, resting on some cotton wool in a finds box. Why had he not known about this place? He could not believe he had never seen it before. His thoughts were disturbed by the young lad standing at the next case.

"'You seen this? It's won-der-ful!" he said.

Nate glanced and nearly choked when he saw what the boy was referring to.

"Wow! Is that a real mummy's hand?" he gasped. "What's it doing here? There aren't any at the Dock Museum!"

The lad looked confused and then shrugged.

"It's all the way from Egypt, you know – where the pyramids are?"

"Dur! Where else would it be from?"

"Good, in't it?" he said, ignoring Nate's sarcasm. "Ya goin' in the reference library? I am! I've gotta find out about some stuff… to do with…"he looked around furtively "treasure!"

Nate raised his eyebrows and followed him out of the museum and into the reference library.

The silence hit him. There were a few people seated at some impressive-looking desks, wooden and with leather tops. A couple of old men were reading huge volumes on lecterns and raised their heads to see who had broken their silence.

A stern librarian sat behind a large desk, surrounded by shelves groaning with books, bound newspapers and other journals. An array of small wooden index drawers stood to attention next to her, and she looked up momentarily and then returned to stamping books.

They crept in. It almost felt like being in church it was so quiet. Nate and the boy sat down at a desk and stared directly at each other. Blue eyes connected with blue eyes, and Nate noticed an amused twinkle glinting in the younger boy's eyes. He couldn't help but chuckle under his breath. A man behind them clicked his tongue in disapproval and the librarian shot a disapproving look over the top of her round spectacles. Both of them suppressed a giggle and the boy whispered, "What are you here for? Not looking for treasure too, are ya?"

Nate thought for a moment and then nodded silently.

"Thought so! Better get cracking then... place closes at five."

With that they set to and began looking in the index cards at the front of the library. Neither asked the other what exactly they were searching for, but they were united in their sense of purpose and worked quietly.

"What's your name?" asked Nate.

"George."

"I'm Nate..."

The two grinned at each other again, in a silent recognition. Nate felt he had known the boy for years. There was something odd about him. He looked familiar but Nate couldn't put his finger on why. He watched him lifting a heavy book down from a shelf, it looked a dreary tome and he didn't envy the boy the task of reading it. George settled down to read, leafing through the pages totally absorbed and oblivious to everything else.

Nate had a sudden brainwave and decided to go to the section where old newspapers were held. He looked around and saw a book case adjacent to the librarian with huge bound books containing newspapers back to Victorian times when Barrow had just begun. He wasn't sure which volume would help, but asked the librarian which paper would cover the late 1890s to the turn of the century. She tutted but directed him to the relevant volumes. He felt like a weightlifter, they were extremely heavy.

He guessed that the gravediggers were dressed from around the turn of the last century and he was heartened to see the few photographs in the papers fitted the style of clothing. It took ages to plough through, but he felt there must be something of relevance in there. Suddenly, a loud bang tore the silence like a gunshot. Flustered readers sighed or hissed in disapproval and the librarian looked up sternly again. It was George, he had obviously discovered the information he wanted.

Again Nate reflected that he looked familiar. He looked closely at the lad and with a nagging air of confusion he recognised some attributes… some he could identify… some that he had himself? But that was daft! He didn't know this kid from Adam! But there it was – he had the same blue eyes, deep set and searching, tousled fair hair, and the ears… those ears which were slightly larger and stuck out a bit… maybe they were related in some way?

He looked back at his book and turned the page carefully, then a second and a third. George came up behind him and looked over his shoulder.

"Cor! Look at that… never knew they found a blooming' sword at Rampside, did you?" he asked innocently.

Nate took a sharp intake of breath and looked at where George was pointing. There at the foot of the page was an old, faded photograph of two men holding an unnatural pose, with… sword fragments in their hands. He pored over the script and read what it said.

Barrow Herald, 12th March 1909
Gravediggers discover Viking sword at popular resort
A badly corroded and fragmented Viking sword was found in Rampside churchyard by Jacob Helm (Sexton) and his son Thomas whilst engaged in digging a new grave in early March. The sword was found approx 2 feet 6 inches below the surface of the dense clay soil, 8 yards west of the boundary wall and 16 yards south of the chancel. The sword lay hidden at the west

end of the grave and a disarticulated skeleton was discovered beneath it.

Unfortunately, the ancient blade was broken by Mr. Helm Junior whilst trying to straighten the sword to remove it from its resting place. "The blade was rusty," alleged Mr. Helm. "It was mighty hard to pull out in one piece," His father asserted that the blade had split when he had tried to straighten it.

Local historians Mr Harper Gaythorpe and W.B. Kendall Esq. agreed the artefact was evidence of Viking settlement in the area and had belonged to a great warrior. The sword is being held by the Cumberland and Westmorland Antiquities and Archaeological Society.

"That what you wanted?" asked George.

"Yep! It'll do for a start… I'll Google it later."

George frowned "You'll what?"

"You know… internet?"

The boy looked blankly.

Nate reviewed him again. On closer examination the boy struck him as odd. He was quaintly dressed in knee-length grey shorts, a knitted jumper and grey socks; he gasped when he saw the shoes… what the h… .? He had on CLOGS! Weird!

Suddenly he looked at his surroundings more closely. No way! It had only happened again… he had flipped in time… what time he wasn't sure – but certainly not his own. The library appeared old fashioned, not a computer to be seen... no electronics of any kind... and that museum... he knew had never seen THAT before. He vaguely remembered Granddad telling him that there had been a perfectly good one in the library at Ramsden Square – and said he couldn't have thought of a more ridiculous site for a museum than the Dock Museum, which was built over a graving dock. But that was Granddad for you – he didn't like too much change. He had described the glass cases and the museum, telling him that he had spent many an hour there as a boy.

They reached the bottom of the stairs and George ran towards the door. He turned and his piercing blue eyes bored into him. A sudden dawning of realisation broke over Nate like a wave. It couldn't be...

"See you later, Nate!" he grinned. "So long!"

So long... so long... that's what Granddad had always said when he said goodbye!

Nate was left staring at a swinging door. He now knew exactly who George was like! Granddad George! But Granddad George as a kid! What was *that* all about?

He rushed outside to catch the final glimpse of the boy running along Duke Street, narrowly dodging a tram. He turned again and waved, disappearing along the busy street. Nate stood bemused, his eyes prickling with hot tears. It was too cruel to be with his beloved Granddad again – for a whole afternoon... but not to know! How could he be so stupid? That old longing ached inside him again, disappointment washing over him like cold rain on a summer's day. He roughly wiped a tear away and sniffed. He now had to work out how to get home again. It was like being on a piece of elastic – being flipped into one time and then another. The regal statue of Sir James Ramsden, the first mayor of Barrow, surveyed the scene unconcerned. Nate noted that there were railings around the statue which were no longer there in his time. As he did so they appeared to melt away in front of him and the picture around him almost pixilated, like when the computer went wrong. He felt giddy… here we go again…

He closed his eyes tight…When he opened them he sighed with relief. Whatever had happened, he was back in the present! How weird was his life becoming? But more important… would he see George again?

Chapter 14

Seeking the sword

Summer evaporated into golden autumn and the excitement of his adventures had left Nate restless and lonely. He had nobody to talk to or share his theories with – he actually missed Tom and Dolly. He had virtually haunted the abbey to see if he could get back to 1750 again and had crawled through the drainage tunnel umpteen times to no avail. In fact the only evidence of his strange experiences was the solitary raven which seemed to track him wherever he went. At least it wasn't sinister, not like those awful magpies that were always perching on the trees in the garden. His sister was *well* nervous of them and he could see why, with their piercing black eyes and malevolent beaks. She seemed preoccupied too and was forever with those mates of hers up and down to the abbey.

Jeffrey was still in his hiding place and he was safe for the time being! But how Nate would find the sacred sword he still didn't know. He had researched the story of St Oswald at the library and on the internet, but this only served to provide him with more jigsaw pieces to puzzle over – and they weren't fitting together at all. He knew the raven was a sign of St Oswald – but it had also been on the sail of the long ship, a symbol of the Norse god Odin. He was still unsure of the link between them, but the evidence suggested that along with the physical relics of Oswald, the sword with which King Penda had slain him had disappeared too. Nate could only guess that the Viking had nicked it… well, they did stuff like that… as he had clearly seen during the battle, when they stacked the weapons taken from the dead Anglo-Saxon warriors. To top it off, Rampside had once been known as Hramn's Saetr, which in Norse apparently meant Raven's Seat!

Nate had found out what had happened to the sword after the Helms had discovered it. It had disappeared from view some time soon after. What was it the newspaper cutting had said? A couple of blokes from the Archaeological Society were holding it? Eventually it had been presented to the Municipal Museum and was now listed as part of the acquisitions of the new Dock Museum.

So, how did he set about finding something which nobody knew was lost? The old monk had said the sword in the museum was not the real thing. It was merely the rusted old remains of another sword. So who had removed it? Surely not the two historians? Or had they had hidden it because they knew what it really was? Maybe someone was after it… maybe they *had* to save it? Hmm! A lot of maybes there and no real answer! Another trip to the library. Nate groaned inwardly, he had more than enough reading to do for his GCSEs, never mind this stuff. He really wished he could find Dolly and Tom again. Between them they would be able to work it all out he was sure.

Chapter 15

Godi

The young boy was red faced and sweating when he eventually collapsed in the small hovel he called home. The village women were in hiding, probably terrified and wondering what had happened to their menfolk. Godi lay panting on the reed-strewn floor, staring up at the roughly thatched roof. He could just see the night sky through the open hole which served as a crude chimney. He gazed into the dark, terrible images flashing through his head. He could not believe what he had seen and even less what he had done. The red devil had fouled these lands before and struck terror into the hearts of his family and village. Many a seasoned warrior had tried to halt his furious raids on innocent people; he had even attacked the church today. None had succeeded in stopping him. Not even his father. Yet *he* had! He knew that God had been with him and it was He who must have chosen him to succeed where others had failed.

He was exhausted from his race to escape and it took but a short time before he fell into a heavy sleep. Hours had passed before he woke. The daylight streamed through the same hole through which he had witnessed the night sky and warm rays caressed his skin and gently woke him. The hut was empty, but he could hear movement outside. He gasped sharply. His mind raced, wondering whether the Vikings had found him. Quietly he crept to the door and peered through a chink in the wood. He sighed with relief as he saw some of the village women and children cautiously venturing back. As he opened the door they jumped with fear, not immediately recognising him. When he did appear fully, a cry went up from his mother and two of his brothers.

"Godi, is it really you?" she cried, silent tears spilling down her ruddy cheeks.

"Aye, mother, it is me! I am safe…" his voice trailed off as they crowded round him. He remembered those sons, brothers and fathers who would not return and his voice died in his throat.

He was swamped on all sides and answered their desperate questions as best he could. Just as he believed he could stand no more, three of the warriors from his village arrived, bloody and beaten, but alive. Further cries went up from the congregated women and children and the men were reunited with their families. Slowly, another handful of men and boys trudged wearily into the village, engulfed by relieved women and children.

When the commotion had settled down, the cost of the battle could be calculated. Some of the families who had lost their men retreated to their homes, others were comforted by the old folk, and children wept. It was a sad day for the village of Aldingham, half of its men and boys lay dead and as yet unburied at Crivelton. As the day drew on and fires were lit, warriors were fed and wounds were treated; life was returning to normal. The warriors who were left had the unpleasant task of informing the lady that her lord Aldwulf was dead. She bore the news with dignity and retreated into the hall with her house carls and daughters.

An outrider had returned from Crivelton and announced that the Viking raiding party had left as quickly as they had arrived. They had buried their fallen and burnt every building to the ground, setting fire to the crops and slaughtering or stealing the cattle and sheep. In short the countryside was devastated, and the Vikings had made sure that any survivors would find it hard to farm the land quickly. The men decided to return in the morning to bring back their dead to honour them.

That night in the great hall the feasting tables were laden with food, and the honour of their chief was remembered with a marvellous feast and plenty of ale. In the midst of the proceedings, to Godi's horror the warriors celebrated his own part in the battle. He was cheered and hailed as a warrior as brave as Beowulf himself. Songs would be sung in his memory for many years to come and children would whisper his name to ward off evil spirits. He shrank from the attention and his face flushed pink, radiating his deep embarrassment. His mother and brothers were plumped with pride at his feat and his grandfather's blue eyes glistened with tears of contentment. Godi paused for thought and reflected how amazed his father would have been. He began to realise that he had avenged his father's death... without even meaning to. The red devil had been responsible for this on the last raid in the previous summer. Who would have known that he would be the nemesis of his father's killer?

Months passed into years and the Furness coast withstood many raids and battles. Godi grew to manhood and became a skilled warrior, who was indeed named in the sagas of his people. He married one of Aldwulf's daughters and raised a strong, large family of sons and daughters, and he became a just and fair lord. He was able to repel the Viking raiders who plagued the coastline, but then when they came in peace and wished to settle he welcomed them and traded with them.

He never forgot the Battle of Crivelton and as an old man returned to the burial place of Red Hair. The monks had returned and St Cuthbert himself had blessed the church, built almost on top of the Viking's grave. The saintly monk had dedicated a new church at Aldingham, the village named for Aldwulf and the church for Cuthbert. It brought a wry smile to Godi's lips that the Viking's resting place was on holy ground, musing whether he had ever reached his Valhalla.

Time came and went. Godi's time was almost spent and he had words with his eldest son Eadgar, who had settled a homestead a few miles north, called Eadgarley. He told his son to place his bones and chattels between Aldingham and Hramn's Saetr and raise a mound in his honour. Eadgar kept his word and the barrow was raised in honour of Godi the great warrior. Long after Godi had been forgotten, years after the story of his bravery was lost by all but a few, his name was remembered at the coastal hamlet called Goadsbarrow.

CHAPTER 16

REVELATIONS

Life had returned to normal for Tom and Dolly. They began to think that it had all been a dream. Often, when night drew in and they sat beside the fire at Mote Farm, they whispered about their friend Nate, wondering when they would meet again.

Dolly was about to return to the inn. It would be safe now that Swarbrick's gang had disappeared. She was reluctant to return because her father was not wholly to be trusted. She consoled herself that it would not be too far distant until she and Tom were wed. He had finally asked her, as she had hoped, when they returned from the abbey, and she was getting older... at 17 she did not wish to wait too much longer.

As they reached the inn Dolly's heart sank. It looked shabbier than ever and brought back bad memories of the night that they had been captured by Swarbrick. They walked across the yard towards the door. Tom grabbed Dolly's hand and smiled reassuringly as they went in. Their welcome was a cool one. Dolly's father was still ashamed of his part in their imprisonment and had hoped not to see them again.

Time ticked by... relentlessly. Tom had rounded up more of the smugglers and the coast was more peaceful than it had ever been. The small port was busy, but most of the ships passed through without trouble. He and Dolly had called the banns at Rampside church and were due to marry in May. Dolly's father had come to terms with their marriage plans and inwardly was relieved that his smuggling days were over. The marriage approached and all thoughts of their adventure with Nate had been forgotten. They had secured a small cottage half a mile down the road from the church at Moorhead and this is where they would raise their family. They were happy and absorbed in their lives, with hardly a backward glance to the past... and Nate.

Nate had been researching. Weeks of inactivity had spurred him to find out as much information as was possible. Oddly, his efforts had revealed something very strange. His many trips to the archives had turned up some interesting facts which had made him shiver. Tom was well documented and he found his marriage to Dolly in the parish records almost immediately. He tracked their children and plotted their passage through time. They had three and all lived locally in familiar villages. He had not intended to go so far but it did capture his interest and he had to admit to himself that it was compelling.

He left his research on the desk in the dining room, unsure what to do with it. He was lying on his bed listening to music and thinking when suddenly his mother called up to him. He raised his eyes and grudgingly dragged himself off the bed and clumped down the stairs to see what she wanted.

"What's all this on the desk? Have you been going through my family tree records?" she demanded.

"What you on about?" Nate asked grumpily.

"These," she insisted, grasping the bundle of papers and waving them in the air.

"They're mine!" he said bluntly.

"Well, how can they be? They are my family tree documents," she pressed.

"No they're not! I got them from the archives… er… I'm doing a project."

"Really? Well…" her voice trailed away.

"That is so odd! These people…are family," she whispered.

Nate could hear the clock ticking. Each tick resounded and hung in the air.

"Family…" He gulped at the strangeness of it.

"Well… yes. This person here is your great, great grandfather." She pointed to a Robert Rallison. She peeled back the papers to the final one, which had Tom and Dolly's marriage details.

"And these two… are your great, great, great, great, great grandparents. However did you find them?"

"Erm… I don't know… they kind of just appeared," he said sheepishly.

"Well, that is very strange… for you to come upon them randomly. Odd!" Mum shook her head and collected the papers up and handed them to him.

"So which part of the family do they belong to then?" he asked.

"My mother's paternal line… the only truly local branch of the family actually and quite an interesting one too."

You can say that again, thought Nate wryly.

Later on during that grey, damp day as Nate sat in the churchyard at Dalton he went over the amazing revelation about Tom and Dolly. Apparently, they rested in this very place. There was no marker, no stone, most of the gravestones had been moved to the edge of the yard or broken up and placed into a kind of patio. Not very nice… he thought. He had not considered before that Dolly and Tom would be dead. It blew his mind that he had met his great, great, whatever… grandparents. To him they would always be his friends, he could sort of see a family look about them, but he could not easily relate to the idea. What would they think if he told them? He would be able to tell them how their kids turned out, grandchildren and so on… but would it be good for them to know? Anyway, it looked unlikely that he would ever see them again.

He shivered; the dampness had struck through to his very bones. He put his head on his knees and closed his eyes. Lost in thought he hardly noticed the cold wind rustling the last threads of the summer leaves on the bare trees. A twig snapped and intruded into his silence like an unwelcome visitor. Nate raised his head to see what had disturbed the peace of the churchyard.

A shadowy shape emerged unexpectedly from the corner of the church. The dull light muted the figure. He skulked for a moment and then darted from the shadows like a lizard into sunlight. The tall figure gazed unblinkingly at Nate and raised himself, cobra like, to his full height. It was Silas Dixon, the man who had upset Chris so much at the dig. Nate jumped to his feet, alert and wary. He backed up, tripping over the grass verge, trapping himself against the wall. Dixon leaned over him malevolently, like a malnourished vulture. He smiled a self-satisfied, predatory smile.

"So, you are still trying to make sense of this puzzle? You will have no way to solve the mystery now that old fool is no longer here to help you."

Nate glowered at him but did not respond.

"You need my skills… and powers to find that which you seek."

Again no response.

"You cannot move through time without the help of a learned one."

"Ha! Well, that's all you know!" retorted Nate savagely.

The man's eyebrows shot upwards, disappearing into his hairline. A scowl knitted his dark brows.

"You cannot pass through the folds of time – you are not of the bloodline!" hissed Dixon. His mouth was pulled taut across his sharp, short teeth, creating an unsettling, reptilian countenance.

"Dunno what you're on about, mister, you wouldn't believe what I've done!" Nate proclaimed triumphantly.

The man's face drained of colour to a sickly white, like alabaster. His eyes narrowed to slits, his stature swelling sinisterly. Nate flinched and instinctively drew back from him, sensing the threat.

A gust of wind swept between the two adversaries, the trees creaking and swaying ominously. Beyond the church wall a misty cloud emerged slowly, hanging strangely in the damp air. They turned to look at the disturbance and Nate gasped in astonishment as he watched the haze swirl and curl, carving out a shadowy figure.

As the haze cleared the figure of a monk was revealed. Nate immediately recognised him. He exuded serenity and his presence reassured the frightened boy. Silas Dixon on the other hand became extremely agitated, visibly shaking and edging away as fast as he could. Behind the monk another shadow appeared. It was barely visible at first, but for a golden halo of shimmering light outlining its shape. Nate was unable to define the image but it was obvious that Silas was terrified of whatever was contained within.

As he stumbled, cowering in retreat, yet a third image materialised. Nate was transfixed by now and the first shade was now fully identifiable. His eyes filled up as he recognised Chris. He took a huge gulp and cleared his throat. He looked just as he had when he had last seen him, but maybe slightly younger and less drawn. Chris smiled the same wry smile he had sported in life, but remained silent. He turned to face Dixon who was cringing with fear and as he did so the third shadow solidified. Nate felt his stomach drop and every hair on his head stood on end with static electricity. He rubbed his eyes in sheer disbelief.

The third figure was instantly identifiable as Tom Rallison. He grinned at Nate and, with a polite tilt of his head, bowed and stepped back beside the monk and Chris. A dull hum resounded around the churchyard and a throbbing golden glow radiated from the three souls. The effect was uplifting and gloriously happy, making Nate invincible. He turned, facing Silas with new resolve. He challenged him to leave with renewed vigour and to his amazement Silas turned and ran, tripping and falling as he went. He was whimpering like an injured dog and Nate felt a little sorry for him.

He turned to the three spirits, invincible and full of energy. They all smiled at him, reading his inner thoughts.

"Beware, my son, do not be fooled by thy power today," said the old monk. "Thou hast much to endure and overcome and we shall not be with thee at every point."

"Who are you… sir?" Nate was lost for the correct form of address to use when encountering a fifteenth century monk.

"I am Brother John Stell of Saint Mary's abbey at Furness. I am the guardian of the abbey treasure and I am here to assist thee in finding that which is lost. These two goodly souls can help thee but the task is thine alone. Thou must discover the resting place of the true sword, which has long been hid."

"But where can it be? It's supposed to be in the Dock Museum!"

"The true sword liest where the keepers left it," Brother John responded.

"But where…" began Nate.

The monk smiled benignly. Chris and Tom stepped back, fading into a welter of mist, their shapes diminishing to nothing but a whisper. Brother John grew paler, his image shimmered and Nate could see right through him. Finally, a small pinpoint of light gleamed and then disappeared leaving nothing but thin air.

Chapter 17

The substitute

Christmas was on its way and he was going to the Carol Service at St Mary's church at Dalton, mostly because Rebecca was performing. He wasn't keen on going to church normally, but knew he would be able to hide among the congregation of school kids and parents. Secretly he quite liked it, but few of his friends would understand.

The church was a busy throng of people jostling to find seats or to get to their places for the concert. He was bemused by the number of people at the service of special remembrance and felt a lump in his throat as he noticed the star that they had put on the Christmas tree for Granddad. The service was exciting and uplifting, it echoed the feeling he had experienced when he had seen the three spirits in the churchyard.

At the interval he saw his sister run off to meet up with those pesky friends of hers. The place was bouncing with people and you couldn't move without banging into someone. Suddenly he stopped in his tracks, hardly believing his eyes. There just behind his sister was George… Granddad! Crazy! He struggled to fight his way through to reach them. He couldn't believe that *she* had seen George too. He wondered why she hadn't said something... but then he hadn't mentioned it to her either. As he apologised for the twentieth time as he bumped into someone he lost sight of the kids, and as he pushed past more people he spotted another familiar figure. The monk was clearly visible in the distance surrounded by candlelight; the children were with him too.

Suddenly he felt light headed and dizzy, just as he had on the promontory at Aldingham. The air was sucked out of his lungs and blackness invaded his brain, spreading like ink until only a small point of light remained at the centre of his vision. As he drifted helplessly, weightless, he wondered if this was what it would be like to enter a black hole. Fear had dissolved; he floated in this dreamlike state, not caring about anything, until he hit the stone floor with a thud.

He was confused and muddled as he assessed his surroundings. He was surprised that he was still in the church, though less surprised that the people had gone and the furnishings and style were of an older time. He was not alone. There in the nave of the church were two men.

Nate called out but there was no response. Just as in the field when Chris had halted time. They could neither see nor hear him. Fascinated he moved closer. They were bent over an object and were speaking in hushed tones.

They were well dressed in old-fashioned suits, with shirts and ties and sturdy boots on their feet. Both were in their late fifties and appeared respectable. As Nate drew closer he saw a piece of sackcloth spread on the floor. On it lay some pieces of metal. His heart skipped a beat as he realised they were looking at the remnants of a sword... the Rampside sword? The pair were nervous and continually looked around them as though they expected someone... or something... to appear and halt their inspection.

"So, do you truly believe we can replace the sacred sword with this tawdry imitation, Harry?" asked the white-haired man.

"Aye, that I do, Will Jackson's grandson will not speak of it again. Their family have had this sword in their keeping since the old man discovered it in 1855 at Rampside. A small payment will ensure its whereabouts remain unknown."

"But will the museum accept this as the sword found by the Helms?" he pressed anxiously.

"Nobody but the Helms and I have seen it closely. Old Jacob Helm is true to the cause and he will keep quiet. Besides, Bill, it is close enough in age and shape to the sacred sword to pass muster," replied Harry firmly.

"It must suffice then, though I see there are some differences, for instance there is no pommel and it's somewhat shorter than the real sword."

"Few know what it should look like but it is at least the correct age and style for a Viking sword."

The shorter man, with greying hair and coffee brown eyes, smiled as he wrapped the pieces of metal carefully into the sacking.

A noise behind them made Nate jump and for a second he thought they could see him. The one called

Bill seized the package and moved quickly to the church door and disappeared into the daylight outside. As Harry turned to leave a familiar mist appeared, silently spreading its tendrils along the nave, until it materialised into the now-familiar monk.

"My son, thou knowest what to do with Oswald's sword?" he asked.

The man fell to his knees and looked reverently at John Stell. He nodded his head slowly.

"Aye I do, Brother, it is in hand. The sacred sword will rest where we discussed at Goadsbarrow. No-one will suspect it is there…" He smiled dryly. "It does seem a fitting resting place."

"When it is safe I will pass on the secret to my trusted friend and we shall guard it through the ages."

"Be sure that ye do, Harper, for 'tis vital it should not fall into the wrong hands," urged the monk.

Now Nate knew who the two men were – the two antiquarians who had been mentioned in the paper, Harper Gaythorpe and William Kendall, pillars of Edwardian society, engaged in duping the generation to come by switching one important artefact for another. He chuckled to himself. All these years and nobody had even suspected it.

It had puzzled him for a while how the sword held at the Dock Museum had looked so different from its original photograph. The one securely wrapped in a box bore little resemblance to that splendid sword with a tang and pommel. In fact when he had seen it once on display, he had been disappointed. It resembled a lump of rusted metal and did not look at all sword-like. He knew that over time it had deteriorated but he did wonder how it had crumbled to just a hunk of rust. Now he knew! Those two old boys had substituted it.

Blackness pervaded his consciousness again and within moments he was back in the busy church amidst the thronging congregation. As he reflected quietly he felt a thump on the shoulder. He turned quickly, just catching sight of George skilfully dodging the groups of people and darting towards the vestry door. He grinned and waved and then was gone.

Chapter 18

Race against time

He couldn't believe what he had seen, but knew that each step took him closer to finding the sword. He suppressed excited bubbles each time he thought of it and had researched more about the two historians. They had cut quite a dash in Edwardian Barrow and were respected scholars. He was still puzzled why the sword was still lost. Surely Harper would have kept his promise and passed the secret on? He pored over the reports of the sword that he had found on the internet and in the library and it seemed that W.B. Kendall and Harper Gaythorpe were into all things historical.

He had even found a reference to the earlier sword being found by William Jackson. He could see that this could confuse people's understanding of the sword and he was interested to see that it had indeed disappeared, or, as the report put it, "its present whereabouts is unknown". Well he knew exactly where it was! But that didn't help him locate the true sword.

Further reading solved one problem. He discovered that in December 1909 Harper Gaythorpe, engraver, die-sinker and illuminator, and erstwhile historian, had died suddenly from angina, only months after the sword was discovered. Nate immediately wondered if he had not completed the task of hiding the sword, or maybe he had, but had not had time to reveal its whereabouts to his friend.

He wondered, too, why Goadsbarrow had been mentioned. It seemed an unlikely place to hide a sword. It was a small place with a few coastal bungalows and houses, but he couldn't imagine where you would hide something.

Again he found himself wishing that he could speak with Tom and Dolly. He returned to Rampside and Aldingham often, hoping to catch a glimpse of them, but to no avail. Frequently he shuddered with apprehension, as he was aware of being watched by unseen eyes.

It was a bright Saturday morning, not raining for once, but bitterly cold. He had ridden down to the coast road and had stopped for a breather at Goadsbarrow as he had done so many times. He swigged on his bottle of cola leaning against the sea wall and looking inland. A sleek black raven flew past, making him nearly drop the bottle; its movement drew his attention to the field across the road. It hovered momentarily and then finally came to rest on a rise in the field. Nate peered curiously at the bird. It stared back meaningfully and Nate paused. It was as though it was trying to tell him something.

He dashed across the road to the fence and looked more closely at the bird's resting place. There was a distinct hump in the field, not huge but raised a little higher than the surrounding ground. He hopped over the fence into the field and went to investigate more fully. It looked like a long barrow or burial mound. He was excited, he had never noticed it before and all kinds of possibilities crept into his mind. He wondered how old it was and what it might contain, but better still, why nobody had ever excavated it.

He prowled around its edge and looked at its contours, imagining what amazing things could be buried in it. Abruptly the raven flapped its wings and rose into the sky, soaring above the mound and then disappearing. A voice broke the silence and Nate turned to see Tom.

"Oh my God! Brilliant! I thought I'd never see you again! Where've you popped up from?" he cried, elated.

"I have been searching this field for booty. Swarbrick is up to his tricks again and I have heard tell that he has buried his cache here. I was investigating and looking for signs of disturbance when I lost my balance and became hard pressed to keep my feet on the ground... and then I find I am here with thee!"

"Tell me about it!" Nate sighed, shaking his head.

"Methinks I just did?" replied Tom, mystified.

"Oh, forget it – it's just a turn of phrase... anyway I'm glad you're here, where's Dolly?"

"She will be at home, her time is near, she is with child," he smiled shyly.

Nate grinned. He couldn't believe it. Tom's first child was due to be born – the boy who would be his great, great ... The mind boggled. If only Tom knew, he would be gobsmacked!

They exchanged news from the last few months, catching up on the quest for the sword. Tom expressed surprise that the sword had been swapped and he ventured that it could not be coincidence that he was here at this time. Nate nodded in agreement and he suggested they investigate further. Both lads wandered round the perimeter of the mound, unsure what they were looking for. They traversed the mound up and down until they had exhausted every curve. They sat down heavily at the base, leaning against the side. Nate drew a pack of sandwiches, a banana and bottle of coke from his bag. The two shared the sandwiches, which gained higher praise from Tom than the burger had done. However, when Nate handed him half of the banana he recoiled, unable to recognise it. Nate gestured him to try it, which he did tentatively. His worried expression melted and he smiled as he swallowed the last piece. However, he refused to share the coke, remembering the taste from last time.

They felt better once they were full and proceeded to examine the mound once more. They crawled around the edge, feeling the ground for any bumps or lumps. After half an hour of painstaking searching, Tom cried out. Nate scrambled over to him excitedly. There was a small depression at the base of the mound, virtually covered with grass; in the dip was a piece of sandstone, buried so deeply it had become part of the mound.

They dug frantically at the stone, sensing its significance. Tom pulled out his knife and dug around the stone, loosening the earth. After carving out a groove they were able to free the stone. They looked closely at it and found that on the face which had been hidden was a small, tarnished metal plate. The plate was engraved and the detail was quite remarkable. A beautifully shaped bird was depicted and each feather was clearly visible, the eyes, beak and feet stunningly real. The bird was a raven.

The winter night was drawing in quickly and the boys decided to pack up and return at a later date. They had not yet addressed the problem of where Tom would stay, but before they could decide anything a chill wind blew in off the tide. The waves were black and angry and huge dark clouds billowed and buffeted from the bay, bringing with them cold, biting rain. Nate turned to tell Tom that they should leave, when suddenly they saw a man on the darkening horizon. He was striding along the perimeter of the far field, sweeping a metal detector before him. Nate gasped in horror. It was Silas. He dragged Tom to the other side of the mound, pulling him out of sight.

They clambered over the fence, hoping they would not be seen. Nate ran to his bike which was leaning against the sea wall. He turned to speak to Tom and to his horror he saw one, two, three magpies flying out of nowhere, cackling loudly and drawing attention to them. The man stopped and looked across the fields towards them. He began moving quickly and threw down the detector. As if this wasn't enough, Tom began to fade and diminish before his eyes. He was trying to say something as he disappeared but Nate was unable to catch it.

Soon no trace of Tom remained and Nate was alone again. Without a second thought he leapt on to his bike and began cycling along the coast road away from Silas

Dixon. Nate rode as though the devil was in pursuit, without looking back. He skidded as he reached the roundabout. The rain drove him on with the wind roughly propelling him away from the sea and towards Rampside church. He didn't stop until he reached Roose. He gasped for breath as he rode into the drive and put his bike in the garage. He leaned against the wall for a moment and collected himself before he went into the house.

That night his mind was full of questions – none of which he could answer. He looked out of the kitchen window to where Jeffrey was buried. The rain bounced off the bird bath and seemed to proclaim that a secret lay concealed there. A single bird landed on the rim of the bath and stood like a statue for an age. Nate watched as a golden light radiated from underneath the patio. Beads of sweat stood on Nate's forehead as he worried that the light would draw attention to the hiding place. Almost as soon as the light had been emitted, it dimmed and disappeared and all was calm. The bird flew from its perch, being absorbed into the black night from which it had come.

Chapter 19

A discovery

He had slept late that morning, because he had not slept a wink. Mum had been yelling up the stairs for him to get up but he really didn't feel like it. He lifted the curtain to take his first glimpse of the day and saw that it was snowing. Large white flakes fluttered down in feathery flurries, covering the ground quickly. Nate leapt from his bed, excited because a proper snowstorm was rare on the Furness peninsula, so he regarded it as his duty to make the most of it. He pulled on suitably warm clothes and raced downstairs to get breakfast. Everyone except his mother was out. Obviously they were all taking advantage of this extreme weather phenomenon.

He arranged to meet his friend Jake later and they spent some time sledging at the amphitheatre. Although it was cold, by the time they had run up the hill and sledged down a few times they were quite hot and sweaty. They broke for a rest and sat looking over the busy field towards the abbey. The whole amphitheatre was milling with children, busy dragging colourful sledges behind them or flying down the hillside shrieking as they went. It was fun just watching. Jake was always a laugh, they had many adventures together and Nate wondered whether to share his recent exploits with him. He was about to mention something when a swishing of wings distracted him. The sleek, black bird swooped close to his head and both boys ducked to avoid it hitting them. The raven landed gracefully just in front of them and faced the abbey buildings. Their line of vision was drawn towards the cloister range where there seemed to be a kerfuffle going on down there. It was hard to see clearly because of the grey mist which shrouded the abbey and the snow obscured the buildings like interference on a television.

He sat up abruptly and peered hard, trying to make out what was happening. People were running across the cloister range and into the Chapter House. A man was running carrying a package, hotly pursued by a group of kids. He strained to see the children... he couldn't believe what he was watching... it was George... and Rebecca, followed by those two friends of hers! What on earth was she doing? He stood to get a clearer view as they disappeared into the Chapter House.

Suddenly a brilliant light, whiter than snow, exploded from inside the Chapter House, casting radiance across the snow-covered lawn. Nate was taken aback and immediately worried for the safety of his sister. He bolted down the hill, leaving Jake and the sledges behind him. He raced to the perimeter fence and climbed over it, jumping down to the other side. He ran across the grass towards the Chapter House and as he reached the arch at the entrance he was astonished to see the children surrounding a large package on the newly laid snow. Next to them were the monk and George. Clearly something strange had happened. However, he would not find out the whole story for some time. Two other people appeared from God knows where, one was Mr Mason, the old groundsman from the abbey, the old lady he wasn't sure. He felt suddenly out of place and retreated, hiding around the side of the cloister wall.

He watched carefully and became convinced that whatever she was doing was in some way connected to his adventure; after all, the monk had seemingly appeared to her too... and George... Granddad.

Over the next few days he wondered whether she knew his true identity, but did not feel able to tell her. His sister and her friends had become celebrities for a time for finding abbey treasure. She hadn't come clean about the magic... or whatever it was, but he had seen enough to be sure that she was up to her neck in something just as weird as he was himself. However, the distraction had been welcome and had even eclipsed Christmas; but almost immediately he had noticed that the raven was back, more evident than ever, as though it was reminding him that his quest wasn't over yet.

It was snowing again, shrouding the world in a silent, white pall. Trees poked through the white-blanketed world like black, bony fingers, the landscape devoid of life and vitality. He was glad when the thaw set in and life returned to normal again. On the final few days of the holidays he took out the stone with its engraved plaque and examined it for the thousandth time. He rolled it around in his warm hands, luxuriating in its smooth texture and tracing the lines of the engraving with his finger. It felt warm in his palm and vibrated with an invisible power. It seemed to be telling him something. He decided to take his bike and go to the mound again.

It was not without apprehension that he rode along the coast to Goadsbarrow, but he steeled himself to face whatever difficulties were awaiting him. He rode to the place where he had last seen Tom and parked his bike. He walked resolutely to the barrow and stood, hands in pocket, waiting for inspiration. It came in the form of the raven. It slowly fluttered on to the top of the mound and gazed precociously at him, taunting him to solve the puzzle. Nate ran to the top of the mound and the raven stood still, unperturbed by the sudden movement.

"I thought I might see thee here!" called a familiar voice.

It was Tom. Nate sighed with relief. It was only right that he was here to help him solve the mystery and fulfil the quest.

"Art thou still seeking the sword?"

"I am… and I'm glad you're with me to do it!" laughed Nate.

He reached down to his bag and pulled out a short shovel. He had come prepared. The only question now was where to dig?

He pulled the stone from deep within his pocket and held it in the palm of his hand. The two of them looked at it, hoping to find a clue.

The stone vibrated with an unseen energy and it began to visibly move. Unexpectedly, it jumped from his hand and rolled to the centre of the mound, as though it was magnetised. The youths gazed at each other and in silent agreement dived on to the place where it had settled. Nate dug into the mound with his shovel and Tom hacked away with his knife. The stone remained buried at the same spot that it had landed. They dug around it and began to make an impact into the top of the mound. When they had dug at least a metre down, they hit something solid. They looked in excitement at each other; maybe this was what they were looking for.

They loosened the wooden boards that had been revealed. It was hard to manipulate them and they struggled to free them and expose what lay beneath. The planks were broken and they pulled out the slivers and shards of splintered wood. Once clear, they were able to reach into the space below and retrieve the objects concealed there. Nate was sure the sword must be there and anxiously felt about for the sackcloth he had last seen the sword wrapped in. He was shocked. Instead of a sword he heaved a sturdy wooden box from its hiding place. In normal circumstances he would have been elated to discover something which so resembled a treasure chest. However, these were not normal circumstances. He was anxious to find the sword. They both tugged at it, pulling it free. It was many years old, but not what they had expected.

It was remarkably well preserved and they forced it open with Tom's knife. The box revealed an assortment of precious items. There were ancient coins, bars of metal, rings and discs, beads and brooches; a vast array of gold and silver of significant age, in fact a veritable hoard. But not the sword! It was obvious that the chest was not the same age as the treasure, and equally the arrangement of it on the ledge was recent and looked as though it had been made specially.

They closed the lid on the riches and sighed.

"These things are many years older than the box, I conjecture," commented Tom. "Someone has hidden these within, to retrieve later... I think some of this is Swarbrick's booty."

"But where did he get them from? He can't have smuggled this lot, can he?"

"I doubt this, he must have found these and buried them to sell later... yet he can not have come back, for they are still here in thy day," Tom mused.

"Hey! Maybe you nicked him! And he couldn't return!" laughed Nate.

Tom thought for a moment and grinned. "Aye...I would say that be exactly what happened... or will when I return to my time!"

They both laughed at the thought.

They returned to the hole and looked deeper. The ledge the box had been on gave way to a lower level where rows of bottles of contraband rum lined the aperture. Tom leaned in and pulled out the bottles. He almost disappeared into the hole. Suddenly he gave a cry and his legs vanished, Nate leaned over to try to catch him but instead fell headlong into the deeper hole Tom had created on crashing through the false floor. The ground had given way to a funnel-shaped shaft which Tom had fallen down. Nate landed on top of him and for a while they lay stunned. It was difficult to see at first, but as soon as their eyes became accustomed to the dark they were able to recognise a small stone-lined chamber. The dim light from above enabled them to explore the small room. At the centre was a neat rectangular kist, made from slabs of stone, which contained a skeleton. Nate used his torch to cast more light on the scene. Strange shadows quivered eerily as the grave yielded its secrets. Around the edges of the tomb were clay pots, which Nate thought were cremation urns. There were neatly piled stacks of bones, topped with skulls here and there. Where the boys had fallen one set of bones had been disturbed and the skull had rolled away into a darkened corner. They looked at each other in awe, eyes huge circles of wonder as they looked around.

They reduced their voices to a whisper, in respect. Nate carefully picked his way through the bones and the urns until he reached the kist. Tom followed him and peered over his shoulder. In the kist lay a skeleton. Nate instinctively knew it was a male and around him lay an array of grave goods. He took a deep breath; this was as good as any Indiana Jones movie! Next to the skull was a stone, with an engraved plate upon it, similar to the one above. The person who had left the stone above must have placed the one below too, as some sort of marker. Nate was immediately drawn to it. As he reached down it began to resonate with a low humming noise, a pale light emitting from it like a beam of sunlight. The light grew and soon filled the room with its radiance. From within it a figure began to emerge. The companions drew back, afraid. As it became clear the figure grew too and what it revealed was terrifying.

A tall, fair-haired warrior stood before them, ethereal but powerful. He looked fierce and bristled with weapons. He grimaced at them, but it was as though he could not see them, almost like a hologram. Nate was puzzled, the warrior had a certain familiarity about him; but this time he was sure there was no family resemblance. Then it came to him – he was older than he remembered, but yes -it was the young boy who had dispatched the Viking so easily. Tom reached the same conclusion at the same time, and as they did so the young warrior vanished, taking with him the light.

"This gets weirder by the second! So the Saxon boy is buried here… freaky!" said Nate.

"'Tis true, stranger and stranger… but fitting that he is here, protecting Oswald's sword, if 'tis indeed here."

They turned their attention to the grave again, doubly reverent this time, knowing whose bones were resting there. There were cups of engraved silver and bronze, daggers and brooches. At the skeleton's feet lay a decorated shield, at his side a spear and a sword.

"Where is it? It must be here!" insisted Nate.

They peered down. Just behind the shield was a thread of brown sacking. There was nothing for it – they had to move the shield and risk the possibility of disturbing the bones. Carefully Nate reached down and lifted the shield. He brought it out and gently placed it on the floor; it felt brittle and pieces of the corroded metal fractured and broke off.

There, between the leg bones was a package wrapped in sacking and tied with simple parcel string. Tucked in the string was a yellowed piece of paper bearing the emblem of a raven.

"Well, that isn't Anglo-Saxon, is it?" laughed Nate.

"I know not, but it does look fresher than the other items we see here," Tom answered.

They lifted the sacking from its resting place with great care. As they opened the paper they held their breath. Tom unfolded the paper and raised his torch to enable them to read it.

December 1909

To whom it may concern,

If you are reading this note, then it is because I have failed in my duty. This sword is the most sacred and revered; that which severed the head of St Oswald from his body. A sword fashioned by craftsmen of great skill and used for so foul a deed.

The treacherous Norse heathen stole it from the Monastery at Bardney. It was lost, but then was found. It is protected by the Brotherhood of the Raven, placed in this tomb and replaced by another. My fellow Mr Wm. Kendall is custodian and shall be privy to this hiding place. Should ought happen to prevent the sword's safekeeping then Brother John of the abbey of Furness will summon protection against those who would use it for ill.

I wish you well and warn you of those dark forces. That which was lost will be found and shall be united with those treasures held safe in the abbey.

Blessings of Cuthbert and Oswald be upon you,

Harper Gaythorpe Esq.

"Wow! That's him, then, the old historian guy!" gasped Nate.

"Then we must now find the place of safety he mentions. Can he mean the abbey?" asked Tom.

"I dunno… but I have another treasure at home… I've hidden it safe, where nobody will get it!" exclaimed Nate proudly.

They moved to the opening of the mound and began climbing up. It wasn't far and the daylight streamed in. Nate got up first and Tom saw his legs and boots disappear over the rim of the hole. As he pulled himself out and got to his knees a shadow fell across him. He looked up and to his horror, saw Nate struggling, Dixon's hand over his mouth suppressing his cries. He thrashed about; trying to free himself, but Silas Dixon had him in a grip tighter than a boa constrictor. Tom grabbed at Silas but as he did so a wave of blackness washed over him. As he fought the blackness he could see Nate stretching out his hand towards him and calling to him, but he could hear only the rushing of his own blood in his ears.

CHAPTER 20

THE ESCAPE

The snow was driving hard across the coast road transforming it into bleak tundra. Each flake stung the skin and Nate shivered with the cold and damp. There was no protection from the fierce wind and each snow flurry soaked him through. He was tied up in the back of the farm truck, bundled behind boxes and feed bags. He felt every bump in the road and his bonds were so tight he could hardly feel his hands. Eventually, the uncomfortable journey ended. It was dusk and the wind was getting up. He lay for some time wondering what his fate would be.

He was not to wait long. It was dark now and he was shivering uncontrollably. The boxes were suddenly moved and he felt rough hands grab his shoulders and pull him out of the truck. He was surprised to see where he was. Mote Farm was very familiar to him considering his time spent there in the eighteenth century. He was hoisted unceremoniously over the shoulder of the man with the rough hands and taken into the farmhouse.

The interior was greatly changed from when Tom's brother had lived there. Pine furniture adorned the kitchen and the centre piece was a huge Aga… Nate couldn't help thinking that it was far removed from its predecessor, the old fire and side oven. Around the big kitchen table were three other people, Silas Dixon seated at the head, a middle-aged woman and a young man. Nate recognised them instantly. The woman had been at the dig a few times, finally having a disagreement with Chris and parting after harsh words. The youth had also worked on the dig for a while until he too had been sent on his way. A picture began to form. He realised that Chris must have been beset by people sent by Dixon to find the treasure.

"So, young man, we have the sword!" said Silas silkily. He smiled and clasped his hands tightly together.

He looked at the sack-wrapped sword lying on the wooden table, smiling smugly.

"Well! You won't have it for long... we'll get it back!"

Dixon smiled again, shaking his head slowly.

"You and your friends from the past? I don't think so. They have no control and cannot predict when they will slip through time; they will be of no help to you."

"You're wrong, we have other help..." His voice trailed off uncertainly.

Silas laughed menacingly.

"The old monk? Salter? They are gone and can do nothing to assist you. They are no threat to me!"

"Huh! You didn't think that the other day... you were scared! *You* ran!" he taunted.

Silas Dixon scowled at him, pushed his chair back and stood up, banging his hands on the table. Nate flinched but then he smirked realising that he had irritated him.

"Young man! You will regret your attitude. You have the skull and I want it. The sword is powerless without it. Where is it?" He demanded.

"You'll never know, will ya?" snapped Nate.

"Then we will take you somewhere to cool your heels… and reconsider!"

Silas picked up the sword, placed it gently in the Welsh dresser and closed the door.

The boy was bundled into a black car and pushed into the back seat. The woman sat in the back with him, watching him like a hawk, and the youth sat in front with Silas. He turned round and grinned at Nate triumphantly. Although it was dark he could identify where they were going and soon they drove into the car park at the Concle Inn. It was closed and looked desolate and cold; the wind drove the sleet and snow across the yard, stinging their skin as they walked from the car to the door. Nate was dragged along into the old pub. As they reached the bar, Dixon disappeared behind the bar and Nate heard a creaking noise.

The woman pushed him onwards, following the direction of the noise. A trapdoor lay open and a dim light flickered in the basement. Nate was forced into the cellar and he looked around at the inhospitable surroundings. Dixon was standing in the middle of the cave-like cellar, smiling sinisterly.

"You can reconsider at your leisure in these salubrious surroundings. I will leave you a candle… but when it goes out you will be in the dark…and alone. You know what this place was, I suppose?"

"No! You're just trying to scare me! Well, it won't work!"

"Really? Well, I have heard stories about phantoms that frequent this inn… you are sitting in the local cockpit, where many a cruel contest went on. Organised by unsavoury characters, smugglers, thieves and brutes all… who knows which spirits linger on… pray you do not find out!" he tormented.

Despite himself, Nate shuddered. He remembered the smugglers he had encountered with Tom and Dolly and had no desire to meet them again, dead or alive. He remained silent.

"So you wish to stay… then this can be arranged. Call out if you change your mind. I will have the skull and I do not care how long it takes."

With that he turned to leave, his companions following him. True to his word he left a small candle burning, its meagre light casting strange shadows around the cavern. The air was damp and the cellar dusty and piled with crates and metal barrels. Every sound was amplified and Nate's skin prickled with fear. He struggled to escape his bonds but the plastic tie wraps were too tight to move or loosen. It was hopeless; he would never be able to hold out for ever. A scraping noise came from the corner of the room. He sat up and dragged his feet towards his body… What if it was a rat? He hated rats!

The candle flickered as an invisible breeze toyed with the flame. Please don't let it go out, Nate prayed silently. A further noise came from the back of the room in the darkest corner. A figure began to appear. He screwed his eyes tight – he really didn't want to see it, whatever it was.

He squinted through half-closed lids… and could see, not one but dozens of figures. There were dozens of figures milling around the cellar, some fully formed and as solid as he, some wisps of white energy, some translucent and beautiful; all moving and speaking in their own time, oblivious of him. His fear changed into awe as he watched people from past times filter in and out. His eyes were riveted to the pictures until he saw a familiar figure dressed like a highwayman, growing more solid and grinning at him. It was Tom.

His anxiety drained away and relief flooded in its place. Tom was there in front of him as real as he had ever been. Immediately he knelt down next to him and took out his knife, cutting Nate's bonds.

"Cor! I've never been so pleased to see anyone in my life!" Nate sighed.

"Aye and I am pleased to be here to assist you! I have been in this place before… Dolly and I were 'prisoned here by Swarbrick."

"Really! Then I hope you know how to get out of here!" he added.

"That I do! If ye can follow me… we will be out in a trice."

He helped Nate stand up and supported him while he got the feeling back in his legs. Tom led Nate to the back of the cavern and located the exit as he had done with Dolly. They made their way down the narrow tunnel towards the breeze and the light. Nate stumbled after Tom and hoped that he truly knew where he was going. Here and there they had to climb over fallen rocks and soil, and roots from above reached their thorny fingers down, clutching and scratching at them as they passed. It was more difficult and uneven than Tom remembered, but then it was nearly three hundred years since he had travelled through with Dolly.

They finally emerged at the other end, digging their way through the obscured entrance. It was very dark and snow was gusting across the coastline. They crept out and looked around to gain their bearings. Tom looked hesitant. Much had changed, of course, and in the dark it looked even more unfamiliar to him. Nate could see the lights from the Gas Terminal and the town at Barrow, so it was easy for him to orientate his position.

"Where can we go? We haven't got the sword and we need to make sure that the skull is still safe," whispered Nate.

"Methinks we must go to where the sword was last seen – knowest thou where it is?" replied Tom.

"Dixon left it at Mote Farm, before he brought me here."

"Then this is where we must go first!" declared Tom with authority.

It was a couple of miles along the coast, but they would have to travel quickly and unseen. They trudged along the path towards the church, bracing themselves against the snow and wind. Nate went over the day's events in his head. He knew they might be missing him at home but he also knew that he had to retrieve the sword as quickly as he could. Somehow, all their existences were tied up with the sword and the skull...

he knew instinctively that it was hugely important to save these relics.

As they climbed over the fence at the church a familiar car screeched along the road towards them. It was Rob. Oh no! What would they tell him this time?

His brakes squealed as he stopped the car. Before Nate could speak he leaned over and opened the door.

"Get in! Both of you!" he ordered.

Without argument they did as they were told.

Something was different about Rob. He had an air of wisdom about him – not his usual image at all.

"Where is the sword?" he asked bluntly.

Tom and Nate looked at each other in astonishment. It was no good trying to hoodwink him – he obviously knew something.

"How do you know…" began Nate.

"The monk… he sent me," he replied baldly.

"How…?"

"Don't ask… you're not the only one with secrets… and stuff… well you wouldn't believe it!"

Nate smirked. I think I would actually, he thought to himself.

"Tis good that thou art with us, lad!" interjected Tom happily.

"Well, I'm still not sure about you – got up in all that weird gear… what's your story anyway?" Rob asked rudely.

"Hey, leave it out Rob! You wouldn't believe it… or who…" Nate trailed off.

"To be honest… after today I would believe anything you told me! That… that bloody monk! What's that all about? I know you're up to your neck in something -and *he's* in it with you… whoever he is and wherever he's from! Now *I'm* in it too – and I'm not sure I really wanna be!"

The three fell silent and it was Tom who spoke first.

"Well, lad, we needs must make haste and repair to Mote Farm once more! We can hold discourse upon these events at some later date!"

"Huh! In common parlance please… what *is* he on about, Nate? Can't he speak in English?" retorted Rob impatiently.

"He said, let's get going to the farm and talk later!" laughed Nate.

They sped off at a rate of knots along the wet road towards Aldingham. They drove past the farm and parked precariously on the grass verge.

"Where do we go from here then?" asked Rob.

"Into the farm… but we'll have to be careful in case any of those thugs are about – don't fancy running into them again!" said Nate.

"Thou must stay here until we return and be ready to move this horseless cart rapidly on our return… can'st thou manage that?" requested Tom.

"He is beginning to wind me up, Nate! Does he think I'm a numpty or summat?" spat Rob irritably.

"I meant thee no offence lad…"

"And don't keep calling me lad… I bet you're not much older than me!"

"Shut up! We have to get the sword…though where we go from there I haven't a clue!" interjected Nate.

Nate and Tom ran across the road and down through the back of the farm. They crept along the outside wall. A light was on in the kitchen but there was no movement. Nate scuttled along to the door like a commando; he shuffled along to the small window next to it and signalled Tom to move closer to the door. Nate slowly leaned over and took a quick look through the window and into the kitchen. The lad who had been in the car with him earlier was sitting at the table playing on his iPod.

Nate scurried back to Tom and they had a rapid discussion. Nate moved to beneath the window again and hid in the shadows; Tom fixed his hat right down over his face, pulled his collar up and took out a small pistol from under his cloak.

All of a sudden he flung open the door of the farmhouse and stood, an imposing figure in the doorway, yelling fiercely, "Thy money or thy life, churl!"

A horrified scream disturbed the quiet of the night and was followed swiftly by the terrified youth crashing past Tom and out into the night. He ran as though the devil was after him and swiftly disappeared from sight. The two companions fell into peals of laughter, releasing the tension of the last few hours. Nate quickly ran into the kitchen and retrieved the sword, which was still where Dixon had placed it. They hurriedly closed the door and ran back the way they had come, meeting Rob and jumping into the car.

"God! I thought you were never coming! What took you so long?"

"Drive… just drive! Look, there's a car coming… it could be them!"

Without another word Rob revved the engine and set off towards the lane to Scales. He cut the corner and swerved into the narrow lane. The two boys grabbed on to their seats to stay upright.

"You don't need to go that fast, you idiot!" yelled Nate.

"Er… I think you'll find I do! That car is following us!"

Tom and Nate looked behind them and to their dismay saw the car making its way up the lane behind them. Rob put his foot down and the little Fiesta roared off like a Formula One car. He was an erratic driver normally, but something took hold of Rob and he calmly manoeuvred the car like a rally driver. They were placing distance between them and the other car, and as they rattled through the sleepy village of Gleaston. Nate had a twinge of melancholy… Five minutes and they would be at the dig field… if only Chris was still there!

They stormed along, passing the houses and up the hill towards the Copper Dog. They narrowly missed a car pulling out of the pub car park, but pressed on regardless. The car held up their pursuers and they were able to fly through Leece and down to Stone Dyke.

"Where now?" demanded Rob urgently. "We can't go home with it…"

Panic set in. Where could they go? Where was safe? Who could help them?

"I dunno… er… what about the abbey?"

"THE ABBEY!" bawled Rob, "How is that safe? There's nobody there to help!"

"'Tis where the sword must lie… and yet thou must retrieve the skull!" interrupted Tom.

"THE SKULL! That thing you brought from Chris?

"Yeah… we'll have to go home… it's there!" sighed Nate.

"Home it is then… but what you're gonna tell mum I can't imagine."

"Oh, I knew it would be my problem!"

They slewed into the drive and screeched to a halt. As they did so the curtains twitched and someone looked out.

"Get that flaming' hat and cloak off, Tom! Try and look a bit normal! We'll get you in but keep yer gob shut or they'll know summat's wrong with you!" instructed Rob taking charge of the situation.

The three unlikely companions got out of the car, and as they walked towards the front door two magpies flew down from the roof and clipped their heads as the flew past.

"What the?" exclaimed Rob.

Before anyone could say more, Nate gestured towards the end of the road. A sleek black car drew into the street silently and parked, turning off its headlights.

"In… now! It's them," ordered Nate.

Chapter 21

The final resting place

They somehow got away with introducing Tom to the family. Nate supposed they didn't guess he was an eighteenth century Revenue man mainly because you would never in a million years expect to see one in your house! He couldn't help thinking how stoked Mum would be to know she'd met her own ancestor – weird! They distracted her by saying they were all hungry and as she disappeared into the kitchen, disgruntled at having to cook at such a late hour, they went upstairs to Nate's room.

Soon they heard the microwave ping and very soon were eating lasagne and micro chips – quite a good effort for Mum! Tom was again mystified by what passed as food in this century, but he was becoming unconcerned about the strange things he had seen. He was baffled by the twenty-first century paraphernalia in Nate's room – not least the electric lights, which he insisted on switching on and off, and the TV which Nate had put on to obscure their conversation.

Rob looked out of his bedroom window, which faced the street where the car was still parked. They were in a quandary about what to do next. Finally Nate suggested they ask Mum if Tom could sleep over; then at least they could formulate a plan.

Permission was granted, reluctantly it had to be said, but by 11 o' clock they had gone to bed, Tom on the put-me-up in a sleeping bag. He had been horrified by the shower, which Nate had insisted he use, but soon got over it once he had given it a try. Rob had lent him boxers and a T-shirt and the transformation was amazing, he looked like any other teenage boy.

They slept fitfully and woke early. Again Tom was kitted out in Rob's clothing and after much protesting even agreed to relinquish the leather top-boots, which they deemed just too odd to wear in the present. His gear was packed up into a carrier bag to be retrieved later. They breakfasted on bacon and eggs with bread – at least more familiar fare than Tom had thus far been offered.

Mum and Dad were going shopping and Rebecca was off with her friends again to Dalton Castle this time, so the coast would be clear. Nate was worried that once Mum and Dad had left the house Silas and his heavies would try and get in. So they decided to make a break for it before everyone left. Rob was on watch while Nate and Tom moved the bird bath to reclaim Jeffrey. One… two… three magpies flew onto the fence… watching, sinister in their silence. Nate carried on, because he knew they must recover the skull to return with the sword. A flash of black feathers shot across the garden to the fence, disturbing the malevolent magpies and scattering them to the four winds. Their raucous cries could be heard across the close. Finally the finds box was out and the bird bath back in place.

They knew they could not risk going up the lane to the abbey. They would have to pass the car. Nate came up with an idea which solved the problem. He led them to the bottom of the garden and began to climb over the fence into the field below. It was a sharp drop of about four metres, but the shored-up banking had huge wooden struts which they could easily climb down. They proceeded carefully down the banking and into the field. Once in the field they raced along the old railway track which had once led to the iron ore mines, last harvested in the nineteenth century, then through the fields to Park House Farm and then on to Bow Bridge. The sword and skull were hidden in the backpack on Nate's back, but to him it shone like a beacon to all who could see.

As they reached the railway crossing by the cottage a lone raven swooped past them and landed on the gate, as though it was urging them onwards. They ran down the pathway past the Abbey Mill and on to the road. As they reached the car park they abruptly came to a halt. In front of them the scene altered, the railing dissolved and the abbey walls changed. Suddenly, the buildings appeared very different; some melted away, others sprang up, trees shot out of the ground and the abbey transformed into a much smaller and simpler version of the one they knew.

The three of them were fixed to the spot and were fascinated with the scene before them. Before anyone could comment, movement came from the trees along the track. A group of monks, clothed in black habits and carrying a simple wooden box, appeared from the trees. They walked slowly and deliberately, muttering prayers as they went, passing close by the friends but without acknowledging them.

"They can't see us," hissed Rob.

"Yeah, I know… let's follow them… " answered Nate.

The three companions followed at a respectable distance. The monks continued at this pace until they reached the gatehouse. The elder monk at the front knocked at the heavy oak door. They were granted admittance and the little procession disappeared into the abbey.

The boys ran speedily to the door, slipping inside just as the porter closed the heavy wooden door. They all gasped as they entered the abbey building, it was incredible… Nate had always imagined what the abbey would look like, but he could never have envisaged this.

Although it had been daylight outside, the interior was dark and gloomy, lit by rushlights. They passed through a small refectory with a long, roughly hewn table and benches, and a rush-strewn floor. On they went to the nave of the church, again sparsely furnished and lit by beeswax candles; a faint aroma of incense hung in the air and the sweet sound of plainsong drifted through from a body of monks in the chancel. The effect was spine tingling, the eerie sound of the chanting setting every hair on end. The monks came to rest in the chapel at the side of the sanctuary; the coffin was placed on a bier ready prepared by the monks of Furness Abbey. They all fell to their knees in prayer and this continued for some time.

An elderly monk, followed by two others, dressed in white habits entered the chapel from the presbytery and knelt at the coffin too. They arose after some minutes and the abbot spoke quietly to the leader of the black monks, unusually breaking the silence required in the church.

"You have brought the sacred relic with thee?" enquired the abbot.

"We have, Father, as arranged," came the reply.

"That is good, we have prepared the chest to contain the sacred relic."

The monks stood and filed out of the church. The abbot, the black monk and the other two white monks said a quiet prayer and moved to the coffin. A young monk appeared carrying a studded chest; he stood close to the abbot and opened the chest, which was lined with luxurious velvet. The Benedictine raised the lid of the coffin and revealed within it the body of a bishop… and a saint… St Cuthbert no less. Nate remembered that St Cuthbert's coffin had been taken by monks on a seven-year pilgrimage in the north to preserve it from Viking raiders. The body was miraculously preserved, looking more asleep than dead. He reached into the box and lifted from it a white skull. He gave it to the abbot who carefully and reverently placed the skull into the box and closed the lid. He then disappeared into the chancel out of sight.

The pageant of ghostly figures showed them that they were in the right place at last. As soon as they had witnessed the scene, the surroundings began to fade and gradually all returned to normality.

They felt disorientated and dizzy, but before they could catch their breath a loud squawking cry severed the silence, revealing a dozen malicious magpies. The birds swooped from the snow-laden sky, homing in on their targets. The boys split up and ran through the church towards the bell tower. Their progress was arrested by the appearance of Silas Dixon and his cohorts. They seized Nate and Rob easily but Tom managed to pull free momentarily. He grabbed at the knapsack which Nate had taken off and thrown to him and ran as though his life depended upon it.

A frantic pursuit ensued, the young man running through the cloister as fast as he could. The youth who was with Dixon launched, rugby tackling him to the floor. The bag shot from his hands and landed in the snow. Meanwhile Nate and Rob had managed to break free and were racing to his assistance. Nate managed to wrestle the bag away from the youth. He slipped and skidded across the wet grass, running headlong into the Chapter House. He cursed his stupidity as soon as he realised that he was trapped by the walls on all sides; there was nothing for it but to try and climb up to the window and jump down to the other side. Before he had chance to try Dixon pulled him down and wrested the bag from him, knocking him to the ground.

Rob and Tom were apprehended and were powerless to help. Silas opened the bag and removed the skull and then the sword. He was overcome with glee and he laughed manically. Nate thought he would be sick, he couldn't believe they had been so stupid.

As Silas looked at the sword with admiration he inspected the skull, matching the single-sided blade to the indentation at the base of the skull. He grinned, his white skin pulled tightly across his face, his eyes sunken and dark in their sockets, looking like a mirror image of the skull he held in his hand. Suddenly his mirth vanished as quickly as it had begun and he lost every vestige of colour, looking more grey than white.

In the centre of the Chapter House a black raven appeared, sleek wings beating slowly, disturbing the air and causing ripples of energy which they could almost touch. The air was static with electrical charge, blue zigzags of light crackling and hissing around the objects. The raven continued to flap its wings; a great blue light, swelling and surging, surrounded it. Around the blue aura a brilliant white light emerged, bleaching the blue and erasing the image of the raven completely; in its place a wonderful white swan, shimmering and sparkling with divine light. The light drowned the ruins in divine light and suffused them with a warm feeling of joy and well-being.

At the edges of the room figures surrounded them. The monk John Stell smiled and made the sign of benediction. An older monk was standing beside a warrior king, and then Chris emerged. They stood strong and proud, powerful energy humming and vibrating the very walls of the Chapter House like a huge battery. The skull fell from Silas's hands and he dropped the sword as though it was a red-hot poker. He let out a wild cry and ran from the place, pushing past the others, out into the cloister; his companions followed suit and the room was still.

The aftermath was strange and emotional. Nate was elated that they had saved the relics and was relieved that Silas was gone; but so many questions remained unanswered. He and Rob hugged Tom triumphantly and then turned to face the others. The older monk spoke first. He was hard to understand at first, speaking in a guttural, hard kind of English. It was difficult to follow, with only a few words recognisable, but as they listened his speech transformed into a more familiar form.

"My children ye have saved my most sacred of treasures and for this I thank thee all," the elderly man smiled, "Yet ye cannot relax your efforts, for there are more tasks to fulfil, before the treasure is vouched safe. Help will be given, but 'tis your fate to resolve these toils and return the abbey to safe keeping. This is a great gift and yet 'tis a great burden too…"

He made the sign of the cross and stepped back. The warrior king held out his hands for the treasures, uttering not a word. Tom picked up the skull and sword and placed it into his ghostly hands. The king bowed and he too stepped back. John Stell nodded in approval and he fell back in line with his unearthly companions. The air around them wavered and shifted, the images dimming and faltering in a haze. A loud crack of blue energy snapped and they were gone.

Only Chris was left. He looked at Nate with sadness in his eyes and smiled.

"You proved your worth lad I taught you well! But don't think this is over, you've more to do… and more to discover… and your brother. Beware of those who are false, you won't always know them but be on your guard…"

"Will I see you again?" gulped Nate.

"One day… you will, but I have borrowed time to set a wrong right; there will be others who can be relied upon."

He smiled and turned around to walk away. As he did so a white mist shrouded his thin frame and only a faint outline could be seen. Nate took a deep breath and as he turned to face Tom, he knew that he too would soon go. His eyes filled with salty tears and he shivered.

He sniffed and wiped his eyes with the back of his hand.

"What about your stuff... your clothes... at our house?" he asked practically.

Tom smiled.

"I think thou canst keep them as a remembrance... and I have these garments of yours. A fair exchange is no robbery!" he chuckled.

A tear spilled down Nate's cheek.

"Nay, friend, thou must not weep. Thou can be sure that if thou art in peril I shall be not far away... I must return to my time... and Dolly... for the bairn must soon be born..."

They hugged again and Rob shook him by the hand. Tom reflected for a moment and smiled affectionately at his future grandsons. The mist grew and spread, silently surrounding him. He was barely visible and as he ebbed like the grey tide, Nate could not help himself. He shouted, desperately, "Your baby... it will be a boy..." Tom turned sharply, speaking... but without sound, he was diminishing and fading.

"*A boy*!" yelled Nate, "And he's *my* ancestor... so are you and Dolly... we're *family*!" he called, emphasising his words.

Tom looked puzzled and could not make himself heard. Nate could not tell if he had heard what he had said and watched as his image slowly fractured and fragmented into millions of tiny points of light and then was gone.

Chapter 22

Aftermath

The two brothers stood entranced, staring into space for some moments. The whole episode had been totally mind blowing and shocking. Nate was sure he had aged ten years and promised himself to check for grey hairs when he got home. He wondered whether Rob was confused, entering into this weird adventure without the same knowledge that he had gained from his strange adventures. How much would he be able to tell him? How much would he believe?

"What did you mean, family?" Rob questioned.

Nate paused thoughtfully.

"You wouldn't believe it if I told you…"

"Er… I think would!" contradicted Rob haughtily. "There are things that have happened to me recently, that *you* would *not* believe – seriously crazy stuff… people… well, I half don't believe it myself!"

Nate's attention was piqued.

"What you on about? Go on – tell us?"

"It would take too long… I'll tell you on the way home… and our Rebecca… she's something to do with all this too."

Nate raised his eyebrows in surprise.

They walked silently from the abbey, having to climb

over the fence… which they had not had to do when entering. Back then, of course, the fence had not existed. They wondered what had happened to Silas Dixon and his cohorts. He had vanished very quickly but they didn't see where he went. They wondered whether he would re-emerge at some time in the future and whether they would see him again. Surely, everything was settled now the treasures were safe… but the monk had told them they were not yet finished, so who knew what would happen next.

As they walked slowly across the field at Bow Bridge a small branch flew from the other bank, hitting Nate on the shoulder. Both boys looked at where the stick had come from and there, across the river, was a boy. It was a boy in a school cap, coat and short pants… and clogs. His face was red with the cold and he stood feet apart with his hands on his waist, grinning from ear to ear, looking like a strange Peter Pan.

"It's George! It's…" Nate looked quickly at his brother, hesitating, not knowing whether to reveal the true identity of George.

"I know… it's Granddad… like I said, it's all been a bit weird recently!" he shrugged.

They looked over the river; a white mist was emerging from the banking.

"Oh no… don't go yet… "cried Nate desperately.

Rob grabbed his arm.

The boy waved sadly.

"I'll see you again… I promise!" The mist wrapped itself around him and he was obscured momentarily. It cleared and in the boy's place was the old man they knew as Granddad. He leaned on a gnarled old stick, dressed in his beige jacket and trilby hat. He smiled his infectious smile and waved at them again. He stood for some seconds watching them, his old eyes shining with tears. They caught a brief glimpse of the cheeky, skinny little boy who was his alter ego, and who had probably been the key part of his personality all his life. He had reached the grand age of eighty-one, but had never seemed old to them.

Abruptly, another familiar figure appeared behind him. It was John Stell. He beckoned George onwards into the haze and then both vanished from view, leaving only a single white, vibrant butterfly in their place.

The two boys walked home quietly, each immersed in their own private thoughts. Ahead of them they could see Rebecca and her friends; instinctively they knew that she had seen Granddad too and that they all had much to discuss. This business with the abbey treasure included her as well and those pesky kids... and seemingly, Rob too.

"So," asked Nate at last, "what *has* been happening to you, Rob?"

"Well, it all began last summer... do you remember, when the garden was trashed?"

Of course he remembered... that was when it *all* began...

Silently, a black feather fluttered down from one of the trees along the lane unnoticed. As they walked along and discussed their adventures, neither of them saw the glossy shape of a magpie quietly rest on a branch above them. They were unaware of a second ebony magpie, with a flash of blue and white, alighting upon a fence post in the next field. They were oblivious of a third predatory bird perched upon a hawthorn bush.

In the far field, behind some bushes, a figure stood, silently watching. He observed them unseen, cursing under his breath and swearing to himself that they would not overcome him again. This was not the end... it was the beginning.

AFTERWORD

Raven's Hoard is the second in the Out of Time series of stories. The Furness peninsula features heavily again and where possible I have used real historical facts and information. The Cuthbert legends have been extended to include the story of St Oswald, and locating Viking raids around the north-west coast is derived from historical and archaeological evidence. The "hoard" mentioned is imaginary and as far as I am aware no such discovery has been made at Goadsbarrow. The mound exists in the topography of the area but Godi's story is fictional, as is the Battle of Crivelton. However, the two swords discovered at Rampside did exist and the "Rampside" sword found by Jacob Helm and his son lies in the Dock Museum to this day – although its authenticity is not in question as suggested in the book.

The characters of Tom and Dolly are a confection of ideas prompted by family history and the real Tom was in fact a Customs Officer for Furness. Dolly was his second wife, but apparently came from the Concle Inn which was known for being on the periphery of the smuggling trade. Smuggling was greatly reduced by the late 1700s and I like to imagine that my ancestor was partly responsible for this.

Crispin Salter is loosely based around a local archaeologist who was very inspirational and charismatic.

He sadly died but will always be remembered. I have taken certain liberties with the local archaeological community, the "sinister" characters are purely fiction, and bear no resemblance to any real "diggers" living or dead.

I must thank certain people for their assistance in research, access to artefacts and information for the book. The amazing staff at Barrow Archives, the Dock Museum, Barrow Borough Council, Furness Abbey all contributed. Once again I am indebted to the research acquired from the work of Alice Leach, Bill Rollinson, and Fred Barnes among others, who provided historical authenticity and information.

The places once again are identifiable and easy to visit, and I would urge anyone reading the book to do so. Rampside church is another lovely local church and worth a visit, as is the majestic Gleaston Castle and its earlier counterpart, Aldingham Motte. We are extremely lucky in Furness to have access to some amazing historical buildings, and I hope that my writing may inspire people to visit and treasure them as I do.

I must mention the two antiquarians, Harper Gaythorpe and W.B. Kendall who are mentioned in the book. They did exist and were at the forefront of early archaeology in the town. They were intended to have a walk on part originally, but strange things happened to dovetail their real stories with this fictional one. Their significance has therefore increased. The Helms existed and I used the actual report by Harper Gaythorpe and the local newspaper reports to glean as much detail as I could about the Rampside sword. This prompted a visit to see the actual sword (courtesy of K. Johnson and E. Critchley) which was a defining factor in the inclusion of the first Viking sword discovered in the same churchyard some years earlier.

Some of the words I use are distinctly northern and might sound unusual to readers not acquainted with them. However, I hope this better illustrates the flavour of the area in which the book is set.

I hope that you enjoy the story and that it will inspire and interest you to find out more about our rich history. The third book in the series is already begun, so the story does not end here.

Gill Jepson

www.gilljepson.co.uk